Enlightened
A Light Tamer Novel

Devyn Dawson

Devyn Dawson

ISBN: 0615717594
ISBN-13: 978-0615717593

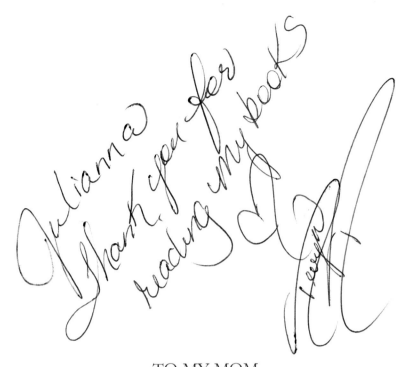

Julianna
Thank you for
reading my books

TO MY MOM

The one person that believed in me long before I did. Never is there a day
I don't think of her. Forever and always, until we meet again…Love your
PDDD

ACKNOWLEDGMENTS

Close your eyes and imagine fireworks, well, you can't read this if your eyes are closed. I have to honestly give credit to my daughter Paris for her encouragement and friendship. It's surreal when your children grow up, and they go from child to friend. My son Hunter for keeping the liveliness in the house. He is my go to for 'is this cool' questions.

To all of the people that have Tweeted and reposted on Facebook about my books and giveaways. For everyone that has written a review, I appreciate every word. To every fan that has emailed me about writing books or to ask about a character. I am humbled by your praise.

Thank you, to my sister for telling me one time when I was a child that writers are artists too.

My friends that have all listened to me talk about characters as if they're real. I appreciate your friendship and thanks for not having me committed…yet.

To my husband Mike for understanding my obsession with watching Sons of Anarchy episodes over and over… it makes me creative, I swear! I find this funny since my books are nothing like SOA.

To all of my author friends for pimping my books. I am grateful to everyone that blogs about books, you really do make authors look good.

CHAPTER 1. ALCHEMY

"The sooner everyone takes their seat, the sooner I can start our morning. You'll notice your name is on the desk, and yes, that means it's an assigned seat." The Hispanic woman says as everyone looks around to find their desk. I double-check my class schedule to figure out her name. Sonya Raine Alvarez, oh, I bet she is grandma's friend Raine.

"Looks like you're stuck with me kid, no escaping the Amber." Amber says from the chair directly behind me. *Let the fun begin.* I think to myself.

From outside, the school is plain as vanilla, red bricks, one story in a U surrounding a courtyard. There is a smaller version of the school next door. It houses the kids from preschool through sixth grade. All classrooms start to look the same after ten years of school, regardless where you live. There were many fluorescent lights and tacky inspirational posters taped to the walls. Twenty four chairs, divided by four rows, twenty-three occupied. The empty seat is right next to me. I lean over to read the name on the paper, Thorne Woodson. The second bell rings and like magic, everyone sits quietly, not moving a muscle. What are they growing here, Stepford Students? Private school is much different from the public schools I've been to.

"I am Miss Raine and welcome to Alchemy 1. With a show of hands, who has been taught the intricate arts of alchemy by their family?" Miss Raine's tan makes her eyes freakishly bright. One of my friends back in New York has waist length wavy black hair like hers, the guys loved it.

Approximately half the class raises their hand, including my partner in crime Amber. Of course, she has, she's sneaky. The door opens and in walks the Uni-bomber's son. He strolled across the room, his black polo barely tucked into his pants, and barely making dress-code. I'm not so sure about the black leather belt with spikes and a giant metal skull buckle though. His Doc Martens are so loosely tied; he has to shuffle as he walks to keep them on his feet. It's seventeen thousand degrees outside, and he wears a jacket, what a wacko. Everyone watches as he pulls the hood down and Miss Raine motions for the ear buds to be pulled out of his ears. His auburn hair, thick and unruly, gives him the urban skater kid edge.

"Thorne?" Miss Raine asks.

He lifts his head in a reverse nod like an arrogant too-cool-for-school thug. He pulls the ear buds out, walks over to the only empty seat...the one next to me, and sits down. His chair makes an obnoxious sound as he shifts it around and leans over to rummage through his backpack.

Amber takes in a breath and mutters to me "ooo la la". She would think he's hot. "Shhhh," I reply.

"In the future Mr Woodson, you're to be in your seat when the second bell rings. Being it's the first day of class, and you are new to the school, I'll let it slide....today. Don't test my generosity, you'll lose. Understand?" Miss Raine says with annoyance in her voice. Thorne gives another reverse nod, in agreement. She leans over her desk and picks up a folder. "The following students need to come to the front of the class. Amber Edwards, Derrick Douglas, Cecelia Judiarti, Carmen Rodriguez, Damian Shock, Thorne Woodson and Jessie Lucentee. Pack up your things, as you will not be returning to this classroom today."

We all gather our things and line up by the door. The other people in class are whispering to each other. My heart is pounding, and my brain is thinking a thousand and one thoughts at the same time. I turn to Amber and say softly, "Do you know what's going on?"

She shrugs her shoulders at me and stares at the back of Thorne's hoodie. Fabulous, a distracted Amber.

"Students, I'll be back in five minutes...try to control yourselves.

The rest of you; follow me." She turns on her heel and goes to the back of the room and leads us into a storage closet.

They must expect to have an overflow of stuff, for a closet this size. All of us look around curiously, waiting for her to explain why we're in here. The stench of dirty bleach water and moth balls are starting to make me light-headed. Shelves are lining the walls to the ceiling, all glass jars of colorful elixirs. Most are bright, while others look as if they were filled with human organs. I'm not even going to guess what they are.

"What the hell? Between the musty smell and Jessie's Victoria's Secret perfume, I'm going to barf," Amber announces.

"My body spray makes you want to barf? Wow, things you can learn from your friends when you're in a closet," I say and grin at Amber.

Miss Raine taps her toe on the ground. "Ladies, are you finished complaining?" She takes her hand and sweeps it through her hair, exposing a little tattoo on her wrist. "Thorne, turn off the overhead light. There is a string directly above you."

"Hey, it will be dark, he can't do that," the guy I think is Damien says.

"You trying to off some Tamers or something?" Thorne's voice is husky with a slight raspy quality. It made me think of the guys on the cover of *bodice ripper* books (my grandma secretly reads

---

them). His rebel side showing for the second time in five minutes.

Miss Raine sighs in exasperation. "You Light Tamers are all the same. Do you have any idea how many times I've explained this? Trust me; you won't be disturbed by any Dark Ones in here. This room is enchanted, and if they'd tell you at a younger age, you'd know better. But *no*, you think the alchemist is an idiot. Now, Mr Woodson, *please* turn out the light."

Amber takes her fingers in the shape of a gun and fake shoots Miss Raine in the back. We stifle giggles only to be shot right back…with Miss Raine's stink eye. Thorne reaches up and pulls the string. Amber and I are armed with our fancy pink flashlights Caleb insisted we carry with us. The teacher shakes her head in disbelief at us. Looking up, we gasp at the never ending supply of potions. Many of the jars are glowing as if filled with a thousand lightning bugs.

"What's up with the jars?" I ask.

"Why are we still standing in a closet, is what I want to know," Amber says as she gnaws on her cuticle.

"We are about to leave the closet Miss Edwards." Miss Raine replies and slides a piece of paper in her white linen pants pocket. Amber shifts to face me and smiles with her teeth gritted and eyes bugging out. "Any time you're at school, everyone is protected from the Dark Ones. By the time this class is over, you'll know how to create the same enchantment for protection."

"You realize working with chemicals is hazardous to my nails. This is bunk." Carmen says as she tucks her short curly hair behind her ear. Her perfect French manicure is highlighted by her dark tan.

I watch as Amber watches Thorne watching Carmen and feel the dread of a love triangle brewing.

"She looks like a tan version of Selena Gomez without extensions, doesn't she?" I whisper to Amber.

She rolls her eyes so far back in her head, and for a split second, she looked like a zombie. "I guess maybe a little, except for the blue eyes. How much do you want to bet she wears colored contacts?"

"You always think everyone has colored contacts on."

"How many Hispanics do you know that have light-colored eyes? I mean, *please*...give me a break."

"Ladies, as compelling of a conversation you're having, we need to get going. Derrick, pull the handle on the mop bucket." Miss Raine reaches in her pocket and pulls out a small vial and tosses it at the bucket as he pulls the handle.

Instantly the wall with all the jars rotates around, exposing an entry to a secret passage. Where's Scooby Doo? All we need now is a ghost and some Scooby Snacks. *Jinkies! Zoinks, how creepy is that!*

"Come on kids, I need to get back to my classroom."

We all walk into a stairwell, down a flight of stairs, through a hallway, and past two doors on either side of the hall. We approach the end, it splits into a T. Turning right, we take the first door on the left. The classroom is an exact duplicate of Miss Raine's room. Taking it in, I see two kids sitting at their desk and a rather peculiar looking man in a monk's robe standing at a podium.

The round bald headed man announces we can take a seat wherever we want. His accent sounds British mixed with a Southern drawl, an interesting combination. Miss Raine leaves, not before telling she'll be back in exactly one hour and thirty minutes.

"Chop, chop, we won't learn anything if everyone is too busy gawking at me in my habit." He says and wipes his forehead with a handkerchief. He clears his throat, which sounds like a cat coughing up a hairball. "I'm Mr Jesse James and no, I am not related to your American outlaw or to a biker." His head tilts to the side as he talks. "This is Enhanced Alchemy. What is it, you might ask yourself? This is an intense methodical form of the art in alchemy. Yes, art. Although your young brain might be thinking science, and I agree; however, it's an art of precision.

I'm not going to bore you to death over the details, you'll understand as the school year progresses. In your desk, you'll find a journal and a textbook. Please pull them out and personalize them. They are yours to keep."

The sound of books slapping the desk fills the room. "Excuse me Mr James, I thought all of our books are electronic textbooks for our I-pads. We have to lug around this giant book?" I ask while clicking the end of my ink-pen over and over nervously.

He gives me an annoyed look. "Yes, Miss Lucentee, you have to *carry* a school book, just like the old days," he says sharply. "Everyone, open your book, and I want you to read the first chapter. You have five minutes to read it and then you'll take a test." We all make a sound of aggravation.

"Can you believe this guy? What a douchebag, that was totally rude of him," Amber says. She picked the seat behind me so I can hear her commentary about the class.

"Less talking and more reading Miss Edwards."

"Like I said, douche," she whispers to the back of my head. I mentally pray he didn't hear her. I hunch over my book trying to let my hair fall into a curtain so Mr James won't talk to me again.

Alchemy (al-kuh-mee)

Noun, plural alchemies

A form of chemistry practiced in Renaissance time. The art of transmuting baser metals into gold.

The use of chemicals for magical elements. The art of mixing compounds into potions for healing.

The chapter is four pages long, but promises by the end of the book, we'd be able to identify and create potions. I'll be lucky not to cause an explosion by the end of the book. I look over and note Thorne never opened his book. I wonder if Mr James will say anything.

"Miss Lucentee, take one and pass them on," I grab the stack and give it to Amber. I see Thorne is smirking in my direction. I shift quickly and stare down at my test. I miss the announcement to start.

Five minutes later I get up to hand my work to the teacher. As I turn to go back to my desk, I run smack into Thorne. *Good going grace.* "Sorry, I have a clumsy gene."

"No sweat," he replies and winks at me. *Did he just wink? No, it's my imagination. Maybe I know him through my grandma. I'd remember him...wouldn't I?* His rugged look works for him. Amber's going to have a field day with his eyes once she sees they're gray. Deep and crystal clear with long black eyelashes. *Why do guys always have great eyelashes and girls get stuck with wimpy flimsy ones?* He is staring back at me, and for a moment, I forget what I'm doing. *I bet he's a terrific kisser with his perfect lips. Oops, why did I say that...think that?*

Derrick is the last to turn in his test. I hate being last; I always feel everyone thinks I'm stupid. Mom would say, someone has to be last. True, but it doesn't make me feel better.

"I am pleased to inform everyone that all of you passed the test with a 100. For a reward, I'm going give you four chapters to read tonight instead of two."

"What the hell?" Amber mutters.

"Oh no Miss Edwards, hell is college," says Mr James. "I'm going to teach you how to make a protection potion. It won't be hard, and I'll give you the ingredients to take home. You will be given a pop quiz later week. I'll grade you on both finesse and speed. Mr Woodson, it will behoove you to practice and actually *read* the chapters. Form a single file line by the back door. We're going to the lab."

"Hey, I need your help," Amber says.

This can't be good. "With what?"

"I'm going to make out with Thorne today."

Breathe in. "Wow, that's ambitious."

"I'm freakin' serious. Look at him, he's all sexified in his hoodie and I think it'll make a statement."

"Statement?"

"I've never talked to anyone at this school other than Caleb. Now you're here, I don't want people to think I went soft over the summer. You know, hanging out with the gorgeous new girl takes away my edge. He'll prove to everyone that I'm still bad-ass."

"You think I'm gorgeous, ah that's sweet? I don't believe the bad-ass for one minute Miss Edwards. Are you planning on kissing him at school?" I study her face and see she is intent on her quest.

Amber shrugs her shoulders and pops her gum. "I don't have a plan, but it *will* happen," she whispers to me. "You only live once right?"

This ought to be good.

Mr James opens the door to the science lab. The difference between this lab and the lab at my school in the Bronx, everything is new and fancy looking.

"Thorne, you want to sit with me?" Amber and I turn in time to see Carmen. She is slithering around him like a snake to its prey.

Oh crap! Amber is going flip out. I glance over at her, she is seething with venom from every pore in her body.

"She better learn her protection spell, because she's going to need it," Amber says through gritted teeth.

"Do you have A lunch or B lunch?" Carmen asks Thorne. "If you have B lunch you can sit with me, I'll introduce you to everyone…if you want."

I nudge Amber with my knee as we sit side by side at our lab table. She is drawing little stick people and what looks like torture devices on her paper.

"I'm in A lunch, I'm already sitting with someone, but thanks."

I look down and see Amber drawing a bubble over one of the stick people and a giant 'Yay!' written inside.

"If everyone has figured out their lunch schedule, we can start on our protection spell." Mr James says. "I'm going to give all of you something else to carry around, just for you Miss Lucentee."

I close my eyes and mentally breathe in to keep my face from turning crimson. He holds up a cardboard box with a girl holding an umbrella on it. Oh yay, my favorite condiment…salt.

"What you might consider ordinary table salt, is simply untrue. It's used in many spells and potions. At one time, salt was once believed to open the entrance to heaven. I haven't any proof either way." His quirky accent makes everything he says sound exotic. "Miss Edwards, your brother was in my class two years ago, did he share his wisdom of salt with you."

Amber goes rigid at the mention of her brother; I brace myself for the verbal lashing I'm sure will commence.

"No, he didn't," Amber replied softer than usual.

"I'm always impressed when former students abide by the rules. Everything we discuss in this classroom is confidential. Don't forget," Mr James taps his finger on his chin before continuing with his lecture. "Salt alone can protect you from many elements…but our main concern is the Dark Ones."

Carmen raises her hand to ask a question. "Mr James," she purrs. "Why are they called Dark Ones, it isn't creative? Honestly, it sounds stupid."

"Au contraire, ma petite chou. Your Historiography teacher will explain the history behind the name. What an exciting year you're embarking on," he says and rubs his chunky hands together. "With Miss Lucentee in our midst, it's sure to be a galvanizing year. Even though, you may disagree with the chosen slang for the former *Light Tamers*, the simplicity of the name fits. I must continue to show you how to make a protection spell. I'd like everyone to open up your silver spout on top of the salt and pour some in your hand."

I clinch my teeth as the spout squeals against the cardboard. Salt reminds me of my visits to North Carolina as a child. No one warned me not to drink the ocean water the first time I went swimming. A towering wave knocked me backwards, and I ended up with a mouth full of water. After choking and gagging I threw-up until I had nothing else in me. I shudder at the memory.

"B, oh for cripes sake, you can't go one class without thinking of *him?* Caleb, oh I miss you...I can not make it without you by my side. Caleb, my love, my heart, my everything, I will die if I can't shove my tongue down your throat in the next five minutes," Amber said dramatically.

I prod her with my finger. "Shut-up, for your information, I wasn't thinking about him. I was thinking about the ocean. So....there!"

"Yeah, whatever."

Mr James clears his throat loudly as he holds his salt up in the air. "Salt is a mineral, from the earth and sea. It's freely available and affordable. I want you to stand up next to your table and arm length away from your lab partner." We all stood up and spread out our arms. "Good, before you do anything, I want you to pour a circle of salt all around you and chant this spell. *Salt of the earth, protect me in this sacred circle.*"

"Do we say the words out loud?" I ask. After a minute, of clarification from Mr James, I hold my arm out and spin in place, pouring salt. I whisper the incantation and cross my fingers. *I don't feel any different.*

"Mr Woodson, I want you to stand perfectly still. No matter what you do, and this goes for all of you...don't step out of the circle."

Mr James holds up a small amber bottle, we all turn to face Thorne standing perfectly still in his circle. In the next moment, the bottle whizzed through the air directly at him. Before I have a chance to think about what I'm doing, I fling my hands into the air.

Everything blurred as the vile halted inches from Thorne's circle. *Oh crap! I chazzled, what on earth do I do? My danger vibe kicked-in, and now I'm going to be busted. Shit...shit...shit. Let it go, don't do anything... let it fly. No, take the vial and put it back in Mr James' hand. I'm so going to die.* I jump up and put the vial back in his hand, then scamper back back into my spot. Time caught up and as if it never happened, Mr James looked at the vial in his hand curiously and then over to me. *Don't call me out.* I cross my fingers praying he didn't notice the hiccup in time.

Mr James pulled back as if he's about to pitch a fastball at Thorne. Before I have time to think, he flings the vial at me. I hear a blood curdling scream, and realize I'm the screaming maniac. I cower down on the floor in a squat, my arms are shielding my face. I look around when nothing happens, suddenly realizing I'd successfully made my invisible shield. I didn't actually see that part, but Amber and the rest of the class were yelling things like *wicked awesome.*

"Miss Lucentee, are you okay?"

"You sure have a lot of faith in us. What if I hadn't done my shield properly? You could have put my eye out with that pitch."

His robe rustled as he walks over to me. "I believe in everything you kids do. I'd like a minute with you in the classroom. Everyone else, I want you to practice your speed in making a circle. Dust Busters are up in front of the room, they are for salt only. Suck up the salt and pour it in the tub on my table, we recycle salt. Miss Raine will be here in about ten minutes and don't leave a mess. She does not like dilly dallying."

I better not get in trouble for screaming, he tried to kill me with the damn bottle.

"Do you have a clue how dangerous chazzling is in a room full of Tamers? It was incredibly thoughtless on your part." Mr James crosses his arms in a huff.

Busted. "I'm sorry, it happened so fast, I didn't even think about what was happening. I'm sorry. Please don't tell anyone. I heard that if people find out, I'll be in danger." I've already screwed up, and it's only my first day. My 'this sucks' list will be updated as soon as I get home.

"You're going to be nothing but trouble for this school and your friends, if you don't think before you react." He looks at my face and the hard lines begin to soften. "Jessie, I'm not trying to be mean."

Swallowing the lump in my throat and taking a mental breath, I look up to face him. "I understand, but how did you know?"

"Within the hidden school, there is little we don't know. That isn't to say that there aren't students with abilities we don't know about, but they know not to use them. I'll report the incident, but it's only listed as a time breech. We don't list the exact ability unless it becomes an ongoing issue."

What did Mrs.Ward say? 'The beginning to a smashing school year." Something will be smashed; I'm not sure what. The door opens; Miss Raine looks at us curiously. She gives Mr James an intense stare down before she gathers the rest of the students.

We follow Miss Raine in a single file line, up the stairs and back to her class. Amber is suspiciously quiet, and when it comes to quiet…you don't think Amber.

"Students who had alchemy lab today, you'll go to lab as deemed necessary. Have a brilliant first day. Fate has a way of bringing us all together, and I for one am grateful to be your teacher." She tilts her head with a fake smile plastered on her face.

The bell rings its melodic tone, not the shrill sounds like we had in my old inner city school. Amber jumps up, throws her backpack over her shoulder and hurries to the door.

"Catch you at lunch B, later tater." Amber says as she practically knocks everyone over to get out of the room.

Later tater? Her nickname for me is B, for Bronx. Only cool people get a nickname from her, so she says. I navigate to the door, paying attention not to let anyone touch me. Without looking up, I sense him...Caleb.

"Hey beautiful, how was your first class? I saw Amber charge out with her old chip on her shoulder. I thought we cured her...guess not," Caleb says and takes my hand. The now familiar current runs through my veins.

"It was enlightening, to say the least. You have Alchemy next don't you?" He nods at me and leads me two doors down from Miss Raine's room.

"This is where I drop you off," he says and gently backs me up against the wall. Leaning down he whispers in my ear, sending my hormones through the roof. "I'll be here after class to walk you to lunch."

My heart skips two beats and a chill runs up my spine. "Why can't I think to you? I tried, but I could tell it wasn't working. Did you hear me?"

"They're probably jamming our frequency. You know they have all of their so-called charms. After this summer, nothing surprises me." He leans in and gives me a quick kiss.

"P D A," someone who looks no older than twelve shouts out. I feel my face flush with embarrassment. It's one thing to have Amber tease us relentlessly, but having a pimply-faced kid do it, is totally different.

I shimmy past him and promise to meet after class. Honors English, my best subject.

CHAPTER 2. MILDLY INTERESTING

"Take a seat at any of the pods, think wisely, as it will be your seat all semester," the teacher says. Pod? I look around and see that small groups of four desks placed facing each other around the room. A few of the faces look familiar from the night at Caleb's house. *The night that almost put an end to Caleb and I. The night that changed my life forever.*

"Jessie, come over here and sit with us," Carmen coos. The other two at our *pod*, Caitlyn and Rob, aren't impressed with Carmen's charms. It's apparent, by the way they roll their eyes every time she speaks.

This may jolly well be the dumbest decision of my life to sit here with the three of them.

"Is it natural or from a bottle," Rob asks.

"Huh? Are you talking to me?"

Rob clucks his tongue and presses his lips together. "Your hair…is it naturally dirty blond or do you chemically alter it?"

"Ahhh, natural, although it gets lighter in the summer from the sun." I reply, trying not to sound like an idiot.

"Oh, so tres chic." By the look on his face, I'm convinced he's considering touching my hair.

"You scored Caleb Baldwin I hear. How did you get so lucky?" Caitlyn asks as she continues drawing Japanese anime pictures of our classroom. Her long raven hair and straight cut bangs with black eyeliner make her look as though she's straight from her drawing. "Not that a guy like him would be interested in someone like me, but he is a feast for the eyes."

"Stop Caitlyn, you're beautiful and a little bad-ass. If you were my kind of thing, I'd so go for you," Rob says and flicks a Life Savor on her desk. "Jessie, I'm kinda known around here to pass out Life Savors when I think you need a smile," he tosses a yellow one to me.

I laugh as Caitlyn and Rob banter until the teacher Mrs. Jones decides to quit texting long enough to call the roll. The way Carmen keeps her purse in her lap, and the occasional look down, she is texting too. Thankfully she is more interested in the conversation going on inside of her purse than grilling me. One hundred and ten minutes seem like a lifetime, for one single class.

Sadly, being new to the school and the teacher preoccupied, I sit silently with nothing but my thoughts.

"Hey zombie girl, the bell rang," Rob says as he slaps his hand on my desk.

I stifled a yelp and look up at his laughing eyes. "That was mean."

"I never claimed to be nice. You headed to lunch? I'll walk you to the cafeteria if so."

Picking up my handouts of classroom rules and shove them in a folder. "Oh, thank you, but it's not necessary. Caleb's waiting for me."

Rob fake stabs himself in the heart. "The first girl I ask to eat lunch with me shoots me down like a wild turkey. *All that we see or seem is but a dream within a dream.*"

I raise my eyebrows at him, and give him a sideways glance. "You're quoting Poe, because I won't walk with you to lunch? Nice."

He claps his hands quickly and squeals in delight. "Oh, yay! Another Poe fan. Girl, we are going to get along fabulously," he says as he prances away.

As promised, Caleb is standing in the doorway waiting for me. "I see you met Rob. He has an endless supply of candy. If sugar is an addiction, he has one."

"That's priceless. Yeah, he clued me in about Life Savors." He reaches for my hand, and we walk to the cafeteria. It was only three months ago when I was walking the halls of Madison High School with my best friend Jersey. Neither one of us had a boyfriend, we played it off by making fun of the lovey-dovey couples holding hands. Here I am, being a hypocrite.

The cafeteria looks nothing like the kind we had in the Bronx. The smell of fresh-baked bread and chocolate chip cookies make my stomach growl. Spread across the room is different food stations, everything your heart desires.

"Where do you want to start? I like the salad bar; it has everything you can think of to put on a salad. If you're not in the mood for rabbit food, we can get steak or chicken, whatever. I'm not picky. I'd avoid the Brussels sprouts though, there's nothing that screams hot like a butt smelling vegetable."

I fill my plate with cantaloupe, grapes and a hardboiled egg. "Where's Amber sit?" I ask and balance my plate of food. Scanning the dining tables I finally see her at a table in the corner of the room. She spots me as I walk towards her. "Hey, we can sit here right?"

"Sit already. For gawd's sake, it isn't like I own the table or anything," Amber says. "This is Shawn, she's a junior too."

Shawn flashes me a smile and a half wave. If I were African-

American, I'd wear my hair just like hers. Her giant afro, with caramel colored highlights, bounced up and down as she moved. "Hi Shawn, I'm Jessie."

"Yeah, everyone's talking about you. I wouldn't have guessed you to be friends with Amber." Her deep southern drawl matched her bouncy hair. "Not that there's any problem being friends with her."

Amber rolls her eyes, bored with the conversation. "Hell-O, I'm right here. Tell me how you truly feel," Amber snaps. She pockets a handful of saltines like a kleptomaniac, stuffing them in the side pocket of her backpack.

"Oh, whatever Amber. Jessie here is one of those classy hippie types. She doesn't strike me as the neglected angst-filled teenager."

"Hi ladies, look how lucky I am. I'm able to sit with the prettiest girl in school," Caleb winks at me, "and the cool kids." His plate of salad was barely recognizable with his pile of ranch dressing smothering it. "You're not too good for me to sit with again this year are you Amber?"

"Touché," Amber says as she grabs an imaginary sword from her chest.

"How's operation Thorne going?" I watched as Amber chewed on a carrot nervously.

Caleb swallowed his hulking bite of salad before asking us what we are talking about.

"Wait, you'll see," Amber said and grinned at us. She pulled the wrapper from a giant cupcake decorated in confetti and streamers. "Want a taste before I take a bite?"

"Thanks, I'm good." I grab my hardboiled egg and salt it evenly before biting into it. Amber takes a carrot and runs it through her frosting before popping it into her mouth.

"Ewww," we all said in unison.

"Everything tastes better with frosting. Do you want some for your egg?"

The vibe at the table suddenly changed as Shawn and Amber stare at something or rather someone who was headed our direction. I jumped as a hand grabbed the chair on the other side of me. I recognize the black hoodie before I even see his face…Thorne. He sets his plate of macaroni and cheese and corn down on the table, and then he takes a butter knife and separates the food. Once his food is void of touching, he takes a napkin and folds it just so. Amber watches him like a cat after a mouse, ready to pounce. Without a word, Thorne starts eating his food like it were his last before battle.

"Dude, slow down. You're giving me indigestion just looking at you. Food should be savored, not swallowed whole," Shawn said.

"My mama would swat your hand."

"Good thing your mama isn't here then, huh?" Thorne shot back. "I'm sorry, that was uncalled for. At my old school, you had only fifteen minutes for the entire lunch. You learn to eat fast. Plus their food was gross, not worth savoring."

"What school was that?" Amber asked curiously. If I didn't know better, I'd have thought her eyes turned to slits like a cat.

"Just a school in a different lifetime," Thorne replied demurely.

Shawn and I watched Amber as she sits stunned that he didn't answer her. Caleb, obviously amused with Amber's lack of comeback, happily ate his salad. We chatted quietly about nothing in particular and Thorne finished his mac-n-cheese and ignored our chatter. I watched in amazement as he pulled out a copy of *The Lightning Thief* and started reading.

"Thorne, I don't mean to bother you while you're engrossed in your children's book, but I have to," Amber says sugary sweet. "Listen, there were things that happened this summer and for whatever reason I got stuck with these two." She pointed at Caleb and me accusingly. "I have a reputation to uphold, and you my dear are my solution."

His right eyebrow lifted, and his face broke out in a grin. "That sounds mildly interesting."

"Mildly interesting? I'll show you *mildly interesting*. I'm sorry, but this has to be done," she stands up abruptly and walks over to where he is sitting. He stayed silent, probably curious about the crazy girl with the wild hair. She pushed the table out of her way. He was sitting with his legs stretched out, and feet crossed at his ankles. If I didn't watch her with my own eyes, I'd never believe she is so bold. She put one leg over his lap and both hands over his shoulders as she straddled him. Without warning, she leans forward and kissed him. The book falls silently to the floor as he puts both hands on her waist. People in the lunchroom started to take notice of our table and cat calls began to be chanted. I scoot closer to Caleb, he put his arm over my shoulder and nudges his chair until we are hip to hip. Shawn's mouth falls open, and I'm pretty sure she isn't breathing.

Thorne was incontestably not objecting to Amber. As uncomfortable it's making me, I can't quit watching.

Caleb whispers in my ear that Major Yukmouth is on her way.

"Yukmouth?"

"She retired from the Air Force as a Major, and her last name is Yukkamoth. She is disgruntled from not being a real police officer."

A teacher wearing *smart* shoes and a perfectly starched white shirt and khaki pants marched over (literally) and cleared her voice loudly, causing the two to come up for air. "That is unacceptable behavior, both of you should be ashamed of yourselves. The two of you practically having sex on the lunchroom floor is the reason for detention. I'll meet you both here after school to scrub all of the tables and chairs." Her finger was waggling so hard that her cheeks jiggle. As she walks away, she yells out for us to mind our own business or everyone will be here after school. As though a giant mute button was pushed, silence filled the room.

"How was THAT for *mildly interesting?*" Amber asks as she wipes her mouth with the back of her hand.

"I don't know, can I get an instant replay?" He replied coolly. Without missing a beat, he picked up his book and started reading again.

Shawn and I struggle to contain our laughter. We laugh until tears are streaming down our faces. Every table that was within eyewitness shot was laughing hysterically. What a way to start our first day of school. Between our early morning meeting in Miss Wards office to Amber randomly kissing a stranger. Grandma Gayle is going to die when I tell her about today.

CHAPTER 3. BONDS BROKEN

My next class The Arts is broken up in different segments throughout the school year. It starts with art history for a week, and then it goes into sketching. Several girls asked me about Caleb and what it was like to live in New York. One girl tried her best to sound like a New Yorker but failed miserably. I took public speech classes since the ninth grade to learn how to hide my accent. I thought it worked, but realized it couldn't hide the fact I don't have a southern hitch. *Maybe, this won't be so bad. It'd be so much better if fourth period would get here already. I'm the only dork on earth that wishes Historiography class would hurry up and arrive. I bet girls are hitting on Caleb. I wouldn't put it past that Carmen girl to try to break us up. She's crafty that way. I have a sixth sense about stuff like that. Is the bell ever going to ring? I wonder where the bathrooms are.* The more I thought about the bathroom, the more I fidgeted. I wiggled until my bladder screamed at me that we needed to go and when it says *go* it means it. My hand shot up into the air.

"Miss Lucentee, can I help you with something?" The copper-hair teacher asked. She wore a copper colored nametag that matched her hair perfectly.

"May I go to the restroom?" In that moment, I realized, no one has asked to go the bathrooms all day.

"Let me find out if I can get an escort for you, it's about time for the bell to ring. You can't wait another fifteen minutes?"

I turned 77 shades of red. "Eh, hem, no ma'am, I need to go now."

"Of course you do. Jasmine will you escort Miss Lucentee to the bathroom." I turned quickly to my left to see who she is talking to and almost peed myself when I saw her. Beautiful long black hair, big brown eyes, and skin so bronze that she'd make a perfect suntan lotion model. She is also the ex-girlfriend to Clark, the guy that was bonded to her, but I fell and he caught me, breaking their bond. By the look on her face, she is none too happy about taking me to the bathroom.

Why in the hell does my life have to suck today? Great, now I'll have to worry about her beating the crap out of me in the bathroom. I know a few Puerto Rican girls from Harlem that put the f in fear.

Jasmine turns to me. "Someone told me that you and Caleb are rebound together. How did you do it?" She flips her long hair over her shoulder. "I have to get Clark back. He and I were perfect together, until *you* and that weird Underworld guy ruined it. He'll be 18 soon, and instead of trying to bond to me, he is out making out with every hoochie he can find."

I know the pain she is in. It's just like when Caleb and I kissed and I felt the pain of us being unbound. "I honestly don't know how we reconnected. Have you tried to kiss him?" I followed her as we walked to the other end of the hall. "Fairytales say that true love's kiss will break any spell. Have you tried that?"

Jasmine stops and pushes me into a locker pinning my back to it. I feel the lock embedded in my back. "You're freakin' kidding me, right? This isn't an F N fairytale, you idiot. We're *Light Tamers*, you know…the good guys. I'm in jeopardy of losing everything I've ever trained for and you're over here saying stupid things like *true love's kiss*. I knew better than to ask you. You're no better than anyone else in this school. I don't know why they're making such a big deal out of you. Freakin' faerie-ass." She is so close that we are boob to boob. *Awkward.* She abruptly stepped back and pointed to a light blue door that says GIRLS. "Go…remember, you had to pee so bad you were doing the pee pee dance in your seat."

She has some nerve, 'fairy-ass', what the hell? So much for the sweet girl I thought she was. I didn't bother replying to her outburst and straightened my shirt as I walked into the bathroom. My hands tremble so hard, I barely get the toilet paper off of the roll. *Don't cry, don't cry. No tears, please don't cry.* The mirror threatened to betray me as I look in it. "Shit, is that the bell?" I turn and run out the door, bumping into a girl who was coming in.

Thankfully, Jasmine was nowhere to be seen. *She probably left as soon as I walked into the bathroom. I wonder if Caleb will ditch Historiography.* Like magic I look up and Caleb is standing in front of me with my backpack.

By the look of concern on his face, he knows something is wrong. "Jess, are you okay?" He pulls me to him and wraps his arms around me. It is moments like these, the world stops spinning on its axis and begins revolving around us.

I shake my head up and down. "I'm okay, especially now. What are the chances that we can ditch our next class?"

"Hmmm, since I've never heard of anyone ditching this school, I'm guessing we can't. Come on, at least we have it together. Do you want to go to the library after school? Amber said she'd meet us there after she is finished with detention," Caleb asked. We walked around the corner and down the math hall.

"Yeah, that sounds good. I have to be home by 5:30 for dinner. Good gawd, this class is huge." We crossed the room and took the two back chairs farthest from the door. I pull out a paper and a pen out of my backpack. I watch as the now familiar hooded figure walks into class. *I wonder why he keeps that hoodie on. Amber said it felt like he is in terrific shape, but she didn't get enough time to explore completely. Oh, I did NOT just think that!*

CHAPTER 4. FILII NOCTE

The name on the desk read Mr Ralph Wolfshadow, Teacher Extraordinaire. His portly build fit his last name to a T. His round face hid behind a mask of hair, otherwise known as a beard. He must have it professionally carved and trimmed, or maybe years of practice made it perfectly outlined. He masked his age well, his eyes sparkled with youth, but his leathery nose aged him.

"You aren't paying any attention to me are you?" Caleb says as he flicks a folded up piece of paper to me.

Thorne takes a seat in the front row, next to a heavy-set guy and a girl from Caleb's house. Unable to quit watching, like a voyeur I watch the girl flirt with him. Touching his arm, and giggling, finally I turn away. Oddly, I feel dirty, I want to wash away the seductive way she acted.

Mr Wolfshadow doesn't strike me as a big cuddly kind of guy, if I were to judge by looks alone. His big bulbous nose is enormous compared to his little close together eyes. He rustled some papers on his desk until he obviously finds the one that he's looking for. He stood up in front of the room and before saying anything, he clears his throat. When I say he cleared his throat, I mean he tried to cough a horse out of his lungs. He pulls out a red handkerchief and covers his mouth with it. I try with all of my might not to look at Caleb, as I'm sure we will die laughing. I sense he's about to laugh, if he does, I'll fall over.

The classroom of possibly fifty students is shifting around in their seats uncomfortably. I'm thoroughly convinced that Mr Wolfshadow is giving us some type of endurance test. I can't prove it, but I'm sure of it.

"Eh, hem, sorry about that kids. My allergies kick up when I'm around so many *Tamers*. Your dander is unbearable to someone like me. Never mind, that sounds harsher than I intend." He wads his handkerchief up and shoves it into his pants pocket. My eyes directly go to the bulge he has put in his pants, and I'm confident I'm officially grossed out. "How many of you grew up with the knowledge of *Light Tamers?*" He finally asks.

Caleb and I look around the room and notice no more than five hands go up.

"Okay, how many of you learned about *Tamers* after starting going to this school?" I look around, and half of the class raised their hands. "Interesting," he says and scratches his beard. "How many of you learned about *Tamers* today or the very minimum, this summer?"

The rest of the class, including Thorne and I, raise our hands.

Mr Wolfshadow flings his arms out wide and starts laughing, and not a little chuckle…he practically falls to the ground in hysteria. Caleb senses how uncomfortable I'm feeling. I know this because he reaches over and puts his hand on mine.

He finally finishes laughing and composes himself. "I have my work cut out for me. I'd like to begin by telling you that I am not a *Light Tamer*, but I am an expert about your species." He says as if we're dogs. *He seriously said we have dander, wth?* "Don't get me wrong, I'm serious when I say that the mythology about your kind is particularly interesting. By the time you're finished with this semester, you'll be armed with knowledge. As you know, that is the best weapon on earth. If you can outwit your opponent, you can win. There are a lot of misconceptions out there. Many of you that grew up with the knowledge might be even more at risk than those that didn't know. You see, many truths have been uncovered in the last decade. That means that what your parents have learned is wrong. With a show of hands, how many know the *Vow of the Tamed*?"

Two girls that are sitting next to each other raise their hand.

"That is reassuring, to say the least," Mr Wolfshadow continued.

"At the end of the course, you will take a vow of silence, next year you'll take the Vow of the Tamed. This class will be mostly lectures, so get your pretty little pampered hands ready to take notes. It would behoove you to start taking those notes…now."

I pull out a spiral notebook with butterflies on it. I look over at Caleb's and see its plain green, but he has drawn hieroglyphics all over it.

"Light Tamers are people who have the ability to absorb light from many light sources. Who can name a light source they cannot absorb?"

Caleb raises his hand. "Light emitting diode, or L.E.D. lights."

"Very good Mr Baldwin. When a *Light Tamer* is in good health and well balanced, they can stay in a room with light, without draining it. You're known as a *Tamer* because your body has learned how to be balanced. It will change your mind about mythical stories and the way you see the world. Not all of you are equal; a few of you will never be able to harness your light." At that moment, no one made a sound. "This is life, you ninny's. Look at Zeus and Dionysus, his son and a god too. He invented wine, which makes him a better god than Zeus, in my book." He chuckles at his own admission. "Dionysus had a mortal mother, this is the first recorded mixed race. His father a god's god, and Dionysus merely the god of vine. Do you understand? In the future, you will be able to harness your light and use it for good things. Let's just say, hypothetically that you are a parent one day, and that child becomes sick, you can heal it. You will simply place your hands on that child, and your light will emit from your hands. Simple right?" Yeah whatever. "I bet you're asking yourself why you had chicken pox, or had a cold. Not all of you have a parent that is a *Tamer*. You have to learn how to heal yourself and that comes with building up your immunity. Although, we'd love for you to have the power to heal everyone, and every animal, it simply can't be done. The world is full of balance, and we must learn how to make sure it stays balanced. It may seem to you that there are a lot of you out there, there isn't. You've had the rare chance to go to a school that is tailored to you. This school is for the paranormally gifted."

What the H did he say? I'm so not going to ask. Nope, not going to do it. Why is my freakin' hand in the air?

"Yes, Miss Lucentee?"

"What do you mean paranormally gifted? Are you saying that everyone in this school has a power?"

"Of course not. Everyone in this school is gifted, not powered. There are some who have the ability to read minds, or control insects. Some of the kids have much stronger abilities, but their secret is theirs alone. The younger children are being monitored to make sure they were born with the suspected ability of their family. The school is sectioned out, and you won't know what the others have. You may share some classes together, but you coexist in harmony. The faculty is aware of most of your gifts, and we're equipped to train you and protect you. Tamers that are juniors will take two classes that will consist of Tamers only. You'll take Alchemy, it has other students, but the Tamers are sent to their special class and this class. There are various types of Tamers. Scientists have identified different bloodlines and maybe one day, they'll expose the truth. I can't tell you exactly what they've uncovered."

The Bronx is sounding more and more like heaven. If I could kidnap Caleb and Amber, we could run to New York.

A buzzing sound came from the room speaker. "Mr Wolfshadow, I have a new student for you. I'm sending her your way, so please don't go all paranoid when someone tries to open the door," said the nasally female voice. We all stifle a giggle.

"Of course, Mrs. Pricer." He opens a drawer in his desk and produces another handkerchief to wipe his brow. He takes a silver thermos out of his lunch bag and pours just enough to fit in the little cup attached to the top of it. We turn our heads to the tapping noise on the door. Mr Wolfshadow hustles over and lets the student in. "Pass please," he holds out his hand to receive the note from the office.

"Oh, just what we need, smartass Amber," a girl two isles over says.

I look up in time to see Amber strutting across the room. She eyeball'd the empty seat in front of me and winked. *Let the good times roll.*

"Hey chickadee, I changed my schedule so I can be in here with you lovebirds. You can pay me back with chocolate covered raisins." She joggles around until she finally settled in for the lecture. "I hear this guy knows a lot about *Tamers.*

"I do Miss Edwards, if you'll take out a pen and paper, you can start writing notes."

"How did he hear you?" I whisper to the back of her head.

Amber shrugs her shoulders.

The teacher walks over to the grease-board and starts writing frantically.

FACT OR FICTION

1. Tamers are protected only if they have two parents.

2. All Tamers must bond to another Tamer before they are 18.

3. Tamers that don't bond are destined to be a Dark One.

4. All Light Tamers are good.

5. If the bond is broken, they can never be bound again?

"To the lovely young lady in the second row, third chair; answer number one." Mr Wolfshadow says as he uses his laser pointer.

The buxom blonde with hot pink lip gloss looks around the class before she answers the question. "I don't know, I just found out about Tamers this summer."

"The gentleman on the back row next to Miss Lucentee, can you answer the question?"

Caleb takes a deep breath before answering. "In my opinion, yes we are better protected when two parents are around." I look over at him and give him a reassuring look.

"The answer to the question is actually ambiguous. The protection doesn't matter if it's your parents. You're protected by adults, Tamer or not. Young children don't typically have enough light in them for the Dark Ones to bother them. The threat of Dark Ones isn't overly obvious until puberty. Many kids are surrounded by adults all of the time. Instinct kicks in and kids throw fits about being scared of the dark. Mommy and Daddy give you a nightlight, problem solved. I can bet that none of you hung out in dark closets." The room nodded in agreement. "Think about it, sadly so, there are a lot of broken homes. Studies have proven that two non-Tamer parents are as effective as one non-Tamer or Tamer parent. Puberty is when you become taller, stronger, and all of those hormones make your light irresistible."

"Irresistible, like chocolate and peanut-butter," Amber whispers to me in her vampire voice. "Follow me you little Light Tamer, with your irresistible pheromones."

"What in the hell is wrong with you Miss Edwards," the teacher shouts, making me jump. "Can you keep your comments to yourself until class is over?" Amber moves her head up and down and straightens up in her seat. "If you haven't figured it out yet, I'm not an easy teacher. I will bust your balls if needed." No one makes a sound even though the teacher just said balls. "I don't care if you're rich, or pretty, or the mayor's daughter. I don't care who you think you are. I care about your safety. Shakespeare wrote about people just like you. If I don't teach you about your species, than I have failed. I. AM. NOT. A. FAILURE." His annunciation of each word makes spittle fling from his mouth.

One girl at the front of the class slammed her pen down on her desk as she jumped up with her backpack. "I'm going to see Miss Ward about you. How *dare* you talk like that to the class!"

"Sit your ass down, you little primadonna. Your principal doesn't give two flips if I say BALLS to you. She wants you to be safe, for what reason? I don't know. I don't care. Well, I do care a little. I don't care if you come from a little house, with a little veil of goody-goody, and I don't care what you think. I'm trying to get you to the point that you understand how to protect yourself." We all turned to face the front of the room, giving the girl the chance be humiliated solely.

I'd be on the verge of tears if someone yelled at me in front of everyone. I wonder who she is. I wonder if that girl frets about her big boobs too? It's probably a lousy idea to go up to her and ask her how she feels about her boobs.

"…and that is how you were protected as a child." Mr Wolfshadow said. "Moving forward, who can tell me what *filii nocte* means?" No one raises their hand. "You're killing me here. Obviously none of you has taken Latin. It means, Children of Night, it's also the real name for the *Dark Ones*. The term *Dark Ones* came into play in the mid 1800's. There is a record of a soldier in the Civil War writing letters about the *Dark Ones*. He was a medic and talked about one of the young soldiers turning dark. How is that for a little history? Rarely is the Latin name used." He looks down at his watch, thankfully the day is almost over. "Okay, the bell is about to ring. I want everyone to write a thousand word essay about your experiences as a *Light Tamer*. It's due next Tuesday."

Before anyone has a chance to moan about the assignment, the bell rings.

"Check on my baby before you leave. Make sure he doesn't miss me too much." Amber says as we walk out of class.

"Baby?" Caleb and I say in unison.

"My jeep…my baby…my love…"

I shake my head and reach over for Caleb's hand. "Gotcha, have fun in detention. I'll see you later, right? I'm sure your *Baby* is fine, I'll text you though."

"Later? Oh yeah, I'll be there."

CHAPTER 5. YOURNIGHTMARE2010

It was delightful to drive out of the parking lot of school. I hadn't realized how tense I was all day, not until I sat on the hot leather seat and it felt fantastic. I told Caleb about Jasmine and how she flipped out on me earlier. He told me about how Miss Raine seemed frazzled by the time she had him in class. We laughed about Amber's public display of affection and we practically drove off the road when we talked about Thorne's reaction.

We stopped for an ice-cream on our way to the library, by the length of the line; we weren't original in our idea. *Can you hear me?*

Nope. I nudged his arm for teasing me. *Did I tell you how cute you look in your uniform?*

You did, but you can again.

Our ability to hear one another's thoughts is something that took getting used to at first. Originally he could hear mine, and I couldn't hear him until we kissed, and only when we kissed. We've been working on blocking our thoughts from each other. It's not that we have secrets, but sometimes our thoughts should be private. At least that's how I feel about it. We bonded a few summers ago when I almost drowned at Emerald Isle. Caleb jumped in to pull me out of the ocean, and when he did; his hands started to glow. What he didn't know then, was he and I were *Light Tamers* and he healed me, and we bonded. He was a little scrawny boy and was a bit obsessed with me. He was always trying to touch me, and I was always trying to keep my distance. No one knew what happened, but Caleb figured it out after his mom died of cancer. Two months ago, my mom and I moved to North Carolina to live with my grandma Gayle. New Bern isn't what you'd call the most exciting town to live in if you're under fifty…or so I thought. I'd never had so many crazy things to happen to me in the Bronx, as a matter of fact, nothing ever happened. True, unless you count my dad's OCD and his problem with alcohol. I'd always thought that if I loved him enough, he would change…he didn't. I learned the truth about his alcoholism once we moved here.

My dad confessed to me that he is a *Dark One* and I'm part of the original *Tamers*, making me irresistible to the Dark. To keep him from stealing my light, he would drink. I love my dad, but I think he could have found another way. He's sober now that he left my mom, and he spends his time trying to track others like him. A little more than a week ago, my bond with Caleb was threatened by Erebus, the god of darkness. He tricked Jasmine's boyfriend Clark into catching me as I fell. Since we're all under 18, our bond can be broken if another bound tamer touches us. I don't understand how 18 is such a magical number other than it's when we're considered an adult. I'm not even 16 yet; my birthday is at the end of August. I have two years to keep anyone from breaking our bond.

Today only added to my confusion about what it all means to be a Tamer. We looked at books on mythology to learn more about Nyx. Amber showed up after detention and told us that Thorne never showed up. It only fueled her attraction to him with the bad boy act.

I told grandma about school before mom got home from work. Mom spent six months applying for jobs in New York and only had two interviews. We were here only a week, before she landed a nursing job at a cancer doctor's office. After dinner, I grabbed the dust buster and practiced making a protection circle as fast as possible. How often I'll have a bottle of salt with me, is beyond me. I do what the teacher wants. I don't ask questions because lately I'm afraid of the answer.

An instant message popped up on my laptop. It was from SURFERGRLAMB.

SURFERGRLAMB: "Whatcha doing?"

BRONXLUVRALWAYS: "Pouring salt all over the floor"

SURFERGRLAMB: "Oh me too! I think the teacher is mental."

BRONXLUVRALWAYS: "You think he's mental? What about Mr Wolfshadow? He's nuts!"

SURFERGRLAMB: "I don't think so, I think he's intense."

BRONXLUVRALWAYS: "Are you running a fever? LOL!"

SURFERGRLAMB: "Ha, ha. Do you want to ride with me tomorrow?"

BRONXLUVRALWAYS: "Sure, I'll let Caleb know."

As I typed out my text, a friend request from Yournightmare2010 popped up.

BRONXLUVRALWAYS: "Who is this?"

YOURNIGHTMARE2010: "Your nightmare."

BRONXLUVRALWAYS: "Okay nightmare, I'm hitting the ignore button."

YOURNIGHTMARE2010: "Thorne, from school."

Thorne, as in unibomber Thorne? No way, how would he get my screenname? It's someone else trying to be funny.

BRONXLUVRALWAYS: "Yeah, right."

YOURNIGHTMARE2010: "Seriously, it's me. I don't know how to prove it. Here, I'll send you a picture of me."

BRONXLUVRALWAYS: "No, send me one of your backpack. That will prove it's you."

I see the flashing message from Amber wanting to know where I'm at. I send her one telling her I'll BRB.

The picture Thorne sent was of his shoes and backpack.

BRONXLURALWAYS: "Okay, I'm convinced. You know I have a boyfriend right?"

YOURNIGHTMARE2010: "That was pretty clear since you two are connected at the hip. I wanted to know your friend Amber's phone number or screenname Miss Conceited."

I blushed thirty shades of red for saying it and then him shooting me down.

BRONXLURALWAYS: "OIC - I'll give you her SN. SURFERGRLAMB. How did you get mine?"

YOURNIGHTMARE2010: "I have my ways. I'll ttyl, I want to talk to her before she goes to bed. Do you know if she's online? Can you send her a text and tell her to get online?"

Okaaaaay. Weird. He's so not living up to the bad boy image I have of him. I send her a quick IM and tell her that he'll be friending her.

CHAPTER 6. SECRETS

Mom and I were up early to go eat breakfast together since she will be working at the ER tonight. Amber pulls into the driveway at the same time we do.

"Good morning Miss Tabitha," Amber shouts over the rumbling of her Jeep. Today the doors are off the Jeep making me feel exposed. "Where did you two come from? You smell like syrup, did you have pancakes?"

"Guilty as charged. I brought you a sausage biscuit…two actually," I hold up the brown paper bag.

"Genius! You're the best B, no matter what the other kids say."

"What?"

She pulls out of the neighborhood like we were in a getaway car. I check my backpack to make sure it's wedged under the back seat. "You're so gullible; no one has said anything about you. That isn't totally true. I heard some girls talking about your hair, wondering if you have extensions. It's your hair right? If not, I look like a total ass. Not that I'm not an ass, but you know what I mean…"

"Yes, I'm fully aware of your ass gene. Sooooooo, did you talk to him last night?"

"Oh that, yeah, we talked. We're picking him up on the way to school." Amber grins but keeps her head facing forward. We pull into a neighborhood with a discreet sign that simply reads Kings Row. We take the second street on our right, its vast front yards and tall pine trees reminds me why I don't like cookie cutter houses. They never get the character captured within their walls, not the way a good old-fashioned ranch house. The GPS announces 'YOU HAVE REACHED YOUR DESTINATION' just as we pull up to a simple brick house.

He is standing on the porch with his backpack over his shoulder and impatient expression on his face. I notice he doesn't have his hoodie on today. His Polo fits him snug, showing off his lack of body fat.

"Hey, thanks girls. I'll jump in the back, you don't have to move Jessie," he says and climbs into the backseat.

Amber tosses the paper bag to Thorne, "we got you some breakfast."

I look over at her, and she gives me one of her famous Amber smirks. She did not just give her breakfast to him. It's moments like these that I wish I had telepathy with her. I am, however, thankful that I don't have a ticket to her thoughts. I shiver…scary thought.

Caleb is getting out of his car as we pull into a parking slot. *Okay, I did not see that coming.* Caleb thinks to me as he approaches my side of the Jeep.

Me either. I didn't find out until we were on our way to his house. "Can you help me with my locker? I keep messing up with the combination I guess. I couldn't ever get it opened up yesterday, remember."

Thorne told Amber thank you as he headed off towards the side of the building. Caleb took my hand and led me to my locker. We walked past a girl who looked familiar, but I couldn't place the face. "Was that girl at your dad's house?"

"The girl we just walked past? No, that's Darla, the girl from Union Point. She's the preacher's daughter."

Funny how people look so different when they're wearing a uniform. Gone is her look of superiority, replaced by a look of shyness. "Oh, right. She didn't have anything to say to us today, now did she? That was a strange day, that owl and the lights…too creepy." It was the first time that I tried to put out such a powerful light by draining it. I knew that there were nine more lights, so we'd be safe. Instead of putting out one light, all of them went out and I fainted. I've never had a problem with fainting before this summer, now I do it about once a week.

Down the hall, and walking our direction is Mrs. Ward. Her starched white shirt tucked into her black pencil skirt enhanced her thinness. She could pull off the sexy librarian if she'd pull her hair up in a bun and wore some black framed glasses. A couple of weeks ago, I went to her house for lunch. It was there that she told me she is one of the three Fates. I wouldn't have believed her if she didn't *show* me how she is Fate. What is explained off as coincidence is nothing more than Fate stepping into your life's path and changing it to fulfill another path.

"How was your first full day of classes? I find it fun to watch the eleventh graders finding out about the alternative classes. Your group is my favorite. I love the healers. Especially your breed of healer. This world needs more of your kind."

"I find it hard to believe that all of this was going on right under my nose, and I never suspected it. Teens aren't very good at keeping secrets, and this one is epic," Caleb says.

"Oh that…it's easy, you take a vow, and it clears up that messy gossiping. Where is Miss Edwards this morning?"

Every time she talks, it's as if she has a sinister plan. We tell her Amber went to class; she turns on her heel and walks away.

"What do you think she wants with Amber? I bet she is ticked off about the lunchroom incident," I say to Caleb.

He shrugs his shoulders and walks me to class. Another morning in my secret class, was exactly the same as the day before.

We passed our salt test and were fitted for custom flashlight holsters. That cracked me up, thinking next we'd be fitted with light vests. The second day in the lunch room was uneventful. Thorne didn't sit with us, as a matter of fact; I didn't see him at lunch. Amber said she hadn't heard from Mrs. Ward but she'd stop by the principal's office after lunch.

CHAPTER 7. DRILL

The tardy bell rings and Mr Wolfshadow closes the door to the room. "Pens and papers out and ready to take notes." I hadn't noticed his limp yesterday, but he limped to his desk. He doesn't look like he's in pain so I'm guessing it's an old injury. "Miss Lucentee, did you hear me?"

I look up, caught utterly off guard by the calling of my name. It's annoying that none of the teachers call me by my first name. "No sir, I'm sorry, what did you say?"

"I asked you what the second question was yesterday. You know those little questions that I wrote on the board for you?" He said sarcastically.

I flip my notebook to the page I'd written it down on. "Do Light Tamers have to bond before they are 18?"

"What do you think the answer to that question is?"

"I think the answer to that question is yes, we do have to bond."

"Are you certain? You and Mr Baldwin have bonded, but something happened to you didn't it? Some type of hiccup and you were bound to another student here."

Why is he doing this to me? I'm going to be the freak because I'm bound...this sucks. I'm updating my list tonight. "Yes, I'm certain...well, mostly."

"Mostly? Write this down and store the information inside of your brain. I don't know where, when, or how, the rumors started you have to be bound by your 18 birthday. That is ridiculous. The correct answer to the question is you will be a *stronger Tamer* if you have bonded. What is true is the fact that you can bond to someone of the same-sex. (Someone in the back row made a sound when he said sex.) Yes, Mr Franks I said sex. You're a junior in a particularly elite private school, and you still act like you're 12 when the word sex is said. Give me a break. On with the lecture." He throws his arms around dramatically making me think of a Kung Fu movie I saw with Caleb. "Students that are bound will have the option to go to the Hidden School of Understanding next year. You have to apply just as you would at any university. I'm getting way ahead of myself. Right now, there is a study that is figuring out the chemistry that exists for those that are bound together. They are using DNA tests that can bring people together and a few other things. You don't have to worry your little heads about it though. It's actually quite fascinating." He stopped and poured himself something to drink out of his thermos. He pulled a small box out of his file cabinet and handed it to a guy that was texting in his lap. "Walk around and hand out one kit to every person in the class with the exception of Miss Lucentee and Mr Baldwin. Each kit comes with a small ink pad, one strip and an area to write your name. You will put your thumbprint in the area that says *thumbprint*. Write your student I.D. number instead of your name in the area that says *name*. Once you have done that, take the strip and lick it. You do *not* need to slobber all over it, just lick it." The guy in the back that laughed when he said sex, was now holding his hand over his mouth snickering. Boys can be so obnoxious. "Young man, if you cannot control your puerile self, you will be asked to leave and go to see Mrs. Ward. Now if you don't mind, I'd like to get through today's lesson before class is over."

"Yes sir." The boy replied sheepishly.

"In case, any of you aren't sure what end to lick, it's the one that says saliva. As soon as you're finished, make sure to put the strip back inside the test tube it came from. Miss Edwards, I need you and Mr Cho to take the box of strips to Mrs. Ward. You will be given 4 minutes to complete the task."

I can almost guess what Amber wants to say right now. I bet she is cussing some serious foul language in her head. I turned to see

Caleb's face and can tell he is thinking the same thing I am.

During the four minutes we all talked to each other. Caleb and the guy in front of him were talking about going to the gym and lifting weights. That reminded me that I'm supposed to go to the athletic department and sign up for the weight lifting class. Caleb was on it last year and wants me to join this year. It's a good idea since I haven't signed up for tennis.

A loud boom goes off, and the room is covered in darkness. A cacophony of shrills and panic spread instantly. It couldn't have been more than fifteen seconds and half the class had their flashlights out and shining. One girl up front starts crying and chanting a spell or a prayer. Caleb reaches over to hold my hand, assuring me everything is fine.

"I wonder if Amber is in the hallway?" I look over at Caleb, and he's worried for her too.

"Everyone, settle down. The emergency system is being activated. Do not move from your seats," Mr Wolfshadow demands.

As he talks, a light in each corner of the room came on. They blinked like a strobe light on slow motion. If there were more lights, it would have felt like a 1980's disco. *They did have disco in the 80's didn't they?*

The door flies open, and a frazzled Amber comes in. She rushes over to sit down, and I can see she's upset.

"What happened?" Caleb asks.

"I've no idea. We were walking down the hall, and the next thing you know; it was pitch black in the hall. I had my flashlight, but he didn't, and he was freaking the freak out." Amber's hand was trembling as she held up her flashlight. "I was trying to keep him calm and get us back in here."

I look around the room and see some kids have their flashlight app on their phone turned on. Oddly enough, Mr Wolfshadow is cool as a cucumber. My grandma always uses that saying. "Caleb, look at him, he isn't doing anything. Do you think this is a drill?"

"Everyone, you need to calm down. As you can see, our back-up generators are on, and the lights are working properly. I've received a message that an announcement will be coming soon. Stay seated, and keep your flashlights accessible."

Thorne turns around and gives Amber a thumbs up sign.

"You don't have anything to do with this do you Amb?" I whisper to her.

"Hell no, you're a turd for even asking me." We all jump when we hear a hullabaloo outside of our door.

The door swings open, and a tall man in a red suit stumbles in. He's probably the same age as my grandma; he would look younger if he didn't have a comb over hairdo. "Jesus! Can it be more chaotic? Where is the control panel? Where?" He is undeniably from New Jersey by his accent.

"The control panel is in the next room."

"To hell it is, this is 26 B and the panel is in here." He walks across the room towards Caleb and me. I do my best to slink down in my chair and blend in with the desk. He pulls out a piece of chalk and draws a square on the wall. Before my brain can actually process what I'm seeing, a door appears. The door is no bigger than a medicine cabinet, but the jumble of wires looks never-ending.

Everyone in the class is watching with curiosity as he plugs and unplugs wires until the room suddenly has power.

"ATTENTION STUDENTS, THIS WAS A TEST OF THE EMERGENCY MANAGEMENT TEAM HERE AT PARCA. HAD THIS BEEN A REAL EMERGENCY - YOUR TEACHER WOULD HAVE TAKEN YOU TO AN OUTDOOR GATHERING PLACE. HAVE A GOOD AFTERNOON AND REMEMBER A SMILE CAN MAKE THE DIFFERENCE IN SOMEONE'S LIFE. KEEP SMILIN'." The school secretary announced in her deep country twang.

"You really did think I did something didn't you?" Amber asked accusingly to me.

"Not really, but when I saw Thorne give you a thumbs up, I

couldn't help but wonder."

"It didn't mean anything. What if it did mean something? Do you think he meant something?"

"Class, if I can get your attention. I am pleased with your reaction to the live experiment. We test our Tamers to make sure they know how to handle the pressure of darkness. A few of you were a little timid and daunt, but that is to be expected. It is only your second day of class. Mr Woodson, what was number three on the list I gave out yesterday?"

"Tamers that haven't bonded will turn into a Dark One," Thorne reads out loud. By the expression on his face, he isn't happy about being called.

"What do you think Mr Woodson?"

"I don't know. It seems a little silly to me to think everyone can find their partner, even sillier to think they have to turn dark if they don't." He scoots his butt as far forward he can without falling out of his chair.

"FACT. You are *not* destined to be dark if you don't find your partner. You won't be as *strong* to avoid the temptations the dark provides. Some turn dark by accident. How many of you know one certain way of turning you dark?"

I raise my hand and mentally pray I won't regret it. "Can't you lose your light if you absorb another Light Tamer's light by accident?"

"Yes, and no Miss Lucentee. If the dying Tamer's light is young and vibrant and their mate absorbs their light, they can and probably will become a Dark One. There's a hitch, a simple loophole to that rule. You won't turn dark if the Tamer that dies is at the end of their lifecycle. When you're at the end of your life cycle, your light isn't as strong, therefore, nothing happens." A buzz of voices interrupts the teacher's lecture. "It is easier to gauge if the Tamer is old, but many younger ones that die are at the end of their life."

"What about those of us that don't bond before we're 18?" A boy across the room blurts out.

"You won't be as strong as a pair that are, pure and simple. There are plenty of *Tamers* finding their mate as an adult. One of the teachers here found her partner after she started teaching. We're hoping that with the experiment, they find the compatible mate to help Mother Nature. She can be so temperamental."

Mother Nature is a real being too? Oh, Mylanta.

"Is it *really* plain and simple, or is that what you want us to believe?" Thorne asks suspiciously.

Amber snorted trying to contain a laugh.

"Yes, why wouldn't it Mr Woodson?"

"No reason, just curious if anything in this world is plain and simple."

Mr Wolfshadow rubs his chin in frustration. I can hear Amber's thumbs clicking as she madly taps out a text message. I duck my head to check my lap for messages.

Amber: HE'S SO HOT

Me: Mr Wolfshadow?

Amber: HA! HA!

I've lost track what they're talking about and start willing time to go faster. I send a text to Jersey, my best friend in New York about her Facebook status. She went from single to 'in a relationship' last night. I've decided for my birthday, I want a ticket for her to visit.

"You daydreaming about me again?" I look up to see Caleb standing next to my desk and smiling down at me.

I've learned quickly that the school parking lot is not the safest place. One girl in a red Prius practically backs up into us. Prius driver's have a different type of road rage. They're jealous of cars that have more power. Caleb tugs on my skirt motioning me to follow him to his car. Above the noise I hear Amber yelling at someone to watch where they're going. Thorne's walking with her, but not actually. He wasn't talking to her, and he didn't seem to mind the parking lot bumper car session. They hop into her jeep, and I notice another guy climb in with them. Caleb eases his BMW out of his spot and we get in line behind a tricked out black car. I click the button on the stereo and turn up *Gold on the Ceiling* by El Camino.

"What had you so deep in thought? You seemed lost inside of your head."

"Oh, I was thinking about Jersey. I was wondering if my mom would buy her a plane ticket. We have a 3 day weekend over Labor Day."

"My dad has tons of frequent flyer miles; he is always wanting to run off on a short trip to use them up. I'm sure he can spare some miles to fly her here."

I reach over and move his hand from the gear shifter. Our fingers entwine together, perfect…minus the fact I'm in desperate need of a manicure. "You are the perfect boyfriend. That would be incredible, if your dad agrees."

He takes my hand and pulls it up to his mouth and kisses it. "Oh, I've been meaning to tell you about the dance. I bet we can get permission to bring Jersey with us. The fall equinox is in September, and we get two extra days out of school. This year the dance is on September twenty-second."

"They celebrate the fall equinox? Do you actually think the school will let Jersey into the dance?"

"I don't see why not. They don't technically call it the fall equinox, it's the fall semi-formal. We get fall break earlier than other schools. It will still be hot, but not nearly as bad. Miss Lucentee, will you please be my date to the dance?"

Squeeeeee! I've never been to a dance before. Mom is going to go crazy for dress shopping. "So, that's an official invitation," I say and bat my eyes at him. Luckily we're at a stop light so he can get the full effect.

"Oh it's official baby, its official."

"I'd love to go!"

CHAPTER 8. BOX OF SECRETS

I haven't heard from my dad in a few days. Earlier in the summer he told mom he was going to Greece to study under his mentor Yiannis Melanitis. Originally that was what I was told too. He took mom's emergency credit card to pay for his flight. Mom had finished up her masters in nursing and was looking for a job when our landlord said we had to move. Without dads income, we couldn't find another place to live. We moved in with my mom's mom, Grandma Gayle, or Miss Gayle as she likes to be called.

My dad showed up at our house one night and told me the reason he is an alcoholic is because he is a Dark One. My dad, my DAD is one of *them*. He said, we come from the original family of *Tamers*. My own father is the bad guy. He told Caleb and I about the girl he had been bound too. She died in front of him, and to keep the other Dark Ones from draining her light, he did it himself. He said it was something so natural to do, and it didn't feel wrong. It awakened a thirst for light, one he couldn't fight without the help of a bottle of booze.

Oh, mom might have a dress I can wear to the dance. I'm taller
than she is, but maybe. When times were good, mom and dad
would dress up and go to art premiers. She sold a few of the
dresses to consignment shops when we were short of cash.

I tiptoe to her room on the other side of the house. The plush
carpet masks the sound of my shoes. It comes in handy when
Amber and I sneak to the kitchen for a midnight raid or when I try
to borrow a fancy dress without permission.

I've never been a kid that does a lot of snooping, I've never had to.
I don't typically go through my mom's drawers, not after I found a
slinky see-through nightie last year. It was hard to look her in the
face for almost a week afterwards. The four-poster bed once
belonged to my grandma and grandpa when he was still alive.
When I was younger, I'd sit in the bed and pretend I was a
princess.

Mom's walk in closet looked bare without my dad's clothes. Her
scrubs were separated by color and hung neatly up front. I reach up
to pull the string to turn on the light. The dresses are towards the
back and still in their dry-cleaning bag. One of my dad's suits is
haphazardly hanging on a wooden hanger. I take the sleeve and
hold it to my nose trying to get a whiff of him. "Daddy, please
come back," I whisper out loud. How many nights I would watch
mom get dressed for an art gala and wish I could go with her. I

tried to convince my baby sitter to drive us by the g
the people on the red-carpet. She never would.

Behind all the ordinary dresses is one I've never seen her
It's a gorgeous black floor length gown. *Oh, if she still has those
gold strappy heels they'll go perfectly with the dress*, I think to
myself. Her shoes are stored neatly in their box on the top shelf of
the closet. I pull over plastic storage bin, and attempt to pull down
two boxes of shoes. As I do, I lean over too far and start to fall. In
typical Jessie fashion, I knock down every box on the right side of
the closet.

I rush to pick up the shoes and match them up with their
correlating box. Sitting on the floor putting everything together, I
notice a box on the floor of the closet. It's a wooden box with a
weirdly shaped keyhole. After checking both her nightstand and
jewelry box, I give up looking for the key. The chimes go off
letting me know a door has opened. For whatever reason, I hurry
and put the box back and slide it into the closet.

"Mom, I'm in your room!" I yell out.

Mom is suddenly in the doorway. "Why are you in my room?"
Her tone is slightly annoyed sounding.

"Trying to find all your secrets," I say, trying to be chipper. I hold
up the black dress. "What do you think this would look like on
me?"

.at's this about?" She throws her purse on her bed and starts pulling her top over her head. I can't help but admire the black lacey bra she is wearing.

I wonder if they have anything cute in my size. I'm sure it is too expensive for someone who seems to grow a cup size every year. "They're having a semi-formal next month. Fall break is the weekend of the twenty-second; we get off Friday and Monday. Caleb thinks his dad will give us his frequent flier points to get Beth a flight to visit us." I used Jersey's real name because mom thinks it's a silly nickname. I hold my breath, hoping she'll agree.

She takes off her scrub bottoms, revealing the matching panties. I avert my gaze, embarrassed to have her see me watching her. "Jess, I'm okay with it, but you need to make sure grandma doesn't have anything planned. Try it on," she says and points at the dress I'm still holding.

The dress slips over my head easy enough. The black chiffon sleeves have a dainty silk cuff that should end at the wrist. On me, the sleeves are too short. I wiggle around until I get everything adjusted. I look in the mirror and try to keep from crying.

"Black is such a pretty color on you. Your dirty blonde hair looks so pretty against the black. Even with your tan, the black is set off your hair and your eyes."

I let out the breath I'd been holding, still trying to keep my composure. "I can't wear this. Look at the sleeves, they're too short. I'm sure it's because I have this giant uniboob in the front." I fumble around with the side zipper and take it off.

"Baby, the dress is too small. We'll go shopping this weekend."

"I don't want you to spend all your money on me. Maybe we can find something cheap at a thrift store."

"I want to dress shop with you, my love. You're looking at a newly promoted supervisor, and I was given a sign on bonus. When I applied, they were offering an incentive that if I stay at least sixty days; I'd get a three thousand dollar bonus. If that doesn't make you happy, your dad sold some of his artwork and sent some money for you." She says as she puts on her booty' jeans and a black tank top.

"That's awesome mom! I need a job that does a sign on bonus like that!"

"Go to nursing school."

"Yeah, I don't think I could empty a bedpan. Why did dad send money for me?"

"He's your dad, and he should send money for you. With that said, how about Saturday morning, we take a drive to Greenville and look at dresses?"

"Sounds like a plan." I throw my uniform on haphazardly so I can run and call Jersey. "You want to do just you and I, or invite grandma and Amber?"

"I'm happy whichever way you want."

"Okay, I'll ask grandma tonight." *She won't say no, I know her too well. I better check with Caleb and see if he has asked his dad yet.* I don't think my feet even hit the floor as I ran into my room.

CHAPTER 9. DREAM

I haven't heard from my dad in a few days. Earlier in the summer he told mom he was going to Greece to study under his mentor Yiannis Melanitis. Originally that was what I was told too. He took mom's emergency credit card to pay for his flight. Mom had finished up her masters in nursing and was looking for a job when our landlord said we had to move. Without dads income, we couldn't find another place to live. We moved in with my mom's mom, Grandma Gayle, or Miss Gayle as she likes to be called.

My dad showed up at our house one night and told me the reason he is an alcoholic is because he is a Dark One. My dad, my DAD is one of *them*. He said, we come from the original family of *Tamers*. My own father is the bad guy. He told Caleb and I about the girl he had been bound too. She died in front of him, and to keep the other Dark Ones from draining her light, he did it himself. He said it was something so natural to do, and it didn't feel wrong. It awakened a thirst for light, one he couldn't fight without the help of a bottle of booze.

Oh, mom might have a dress I can wear to the dance. I'm taller than she is, but maybe. When times were good, mom and dad would dress up and go to art premiers. She sold a few of the dresses to consignment shops when we were short of cash.

I tiptoe to her room on the other side of the house. The plush carpet masks the sound of my shoes. It comes in handy when Amber and I sneak to the kitchen for a midnight raid or when I try to borrow a fancy dress without permission.

I've never been a kid that does a lot of snooping, I've never had to. I don't typically go through my mom's drawers, not after I found a slinky see-through nightie last year. It was hard to look her in the face for almost a week afterwards. The four-poster bed once belonged to my grandma and grandpa when he was still alive. When I was younger, I'd sit in the bed and pretend I was a princess.

Mom's walk in closet looked bare without my dad's clothes. Her scrubs were separated by color and hung neatly up front. I reach up to pull the string to turn on the light. The dresses are towards the back and still in their dry-cleaning bag. One of my dad's suits is haphazardly hanging on a wooden hanger. I take the sleeve and hold it to my nose trying to get a whiff of him. "Daddy, please come back," I whisper out loud. How many nights I would watch mom get dressed for an art gala and wish I could go with her. I tried to convince my baby sitter to drive us by the gallery to watch the people on the red-carpet. She never would.

Behind all the ordinary dresses is one I've never seen her wear. It's a gorgeous black floor length gown. *Oh, if she still has those gold strappy heels they'll go perfectly with the dress*, I think to myself. Her shoes are stored neatly in their box on the top shelf of the closet. I pull over plastic storage bin, and attempt to pull down two boxes of shoes. As I do, I lean over too far and start to fall. In typical Jessie fashion, I knock down every box on the right side of the closet.

I rush to pick up the shoes and match them up with their correlating box. Sitting on the floor putting everything together, I notice a box on the floor of the closet. It's a wooden box with a weirdly shaped keyhole. After checking both her nightstand and jewelry box, I give up looking for the key. The chimes go off letting me know a door has opened. For whatever reason, I hurry and put the box back and slide it into the closet.

"Mom, I'm in your room!" I yell out.

Mom is suddenly in the doorway. "Why are you in my room?" Her tone is slightly annoyed sounding.

"Trying to find all your secrets," I say, trying to be chipper. I hold up the black dress. "What do you think this would look like on me?"

"What's this about?" She throws her purse on her bed and starts pulling her top over her head. I can't help but admire the black lacey bra she is wearing.

I wonder if they have anything cute in my size. I'm sure it is too expensive for someone who seems to grow a cup size every year. "They're having a semi-formal next month. Fall break is the weekend of the twenty-second; we get off Friday and Monday. Caleb thinks his dad will give us his frequent flier points to get Beth a flight to visit us." I used Jersey's real name because mom thinks it's a silly nickname. I hold my breath, hoping she'll agree.

She takes off her scrub bottoms, revealing the matching panties. I avert my gaze, embarrassed to have her see me watching her. "Jess, I'm okay with it, but you need to make sure grandma doesn't have anything planned. Try it on," she says and points at the dress I'm still holding.

The dress slips over my head easy enough. The black chiffon sleeves have a dainty silk cuff that should end at the wrist. On me, the sleeves are too short. I wiggle around until I get everything adjusted. I look in the mirror and try to keep from crying.

"Black is such a pretty color on you. Your dirty blonde hair looks so pretty against the black. Even with your tan, the black is set off your hair and your eyes."

I let out the breath I'd been holding, still trying to keep my composure. "I can't wear this. Look at the sleeves, they're too short. I'm sure it's because I have this giant uniboob in the front." I fumble around with the side zipper and take it off.

"Baby, the dress is too small. We'll go shopping this weekend."

"I don't want you to spend all your money on me. Maybe we can find something cheap at a thrift store."

"I want to dress shop with you, my love. You're looking at a newly promoted supervisor, and I was given a sign on bonus. When I applied, they were offering an incentive that if I stay at least sixty days; I'd get a three thousand dollar bonus. If that doesn't make you happy, your dad sold some of his artwork and sent some money for you." She says as she puts on her booty' jeans and a black tank top.

"That's awesome mom! I need a job that does a sign on bonus like that!"

"Go to nursing school."

"Yeah, I don't think I could empty a bedpan. Why did dad send money for me?"

"He's your dad, and he should send money for you. With that said, how about Saturday morning, we take a drive to Greenville and look at dresses?"

"Sounds like a plan." I throw my uniform on haphazardly so I can run and call Jersey. "You want to do just you and I, or invite grandma and Amber?"

"I'm happy whichever way you want."

"Okay, I'll ask grandma tonight." *She won't say no, I know her too well. I better check with Caleb and see if he has asked his dad yet.* I don't think my feet even hit the floor as I ran into my room.

10 GUARDIAN'S CALL

"Good to see you've made it home safe and sound," Grandma says as I walk in five minutes late.

"I'm sorry, we stopped to get some ice-cream, and they took forever." I lean over and hand her one of her favorite treats of all time.

"A mocha-java drink? I'm easily bribable," she says smiling at me. Grandma looks ten or more years younger than she is. Living in the south, we call everyone Miss or Mister plus their first name. Grandma insists that I call her Miss Gayle, as she's in denial that she can be old enough to fit the title of grandma. We've always had a unique bond, either from me coming to North Carolina every summer or because we're a lot alike. "Let's go in my room, your mom conked out on the couch. She has been working so much, she is missing out on living."

The hall to grandma's room is filled with pictures of my mom when she was young, and pictures of me. There were photos of grandma and grandpa's wedding and family I've never met. I don't have any memories of my grandfather; I was young when he died. He was thrown from a horse and another horse stomped on him. His internal injuries were too severe, and he died two weeks later. Grandma still has a hard time talking about him; she tears up and leaves the room until she composes herself. Mom always said they had the perfect marriage, and she wants the same for me one day. Caleb and I'll be that way…I hope.

Her room screams Hollywood drama with its crystal chandeliers and white furniture that pop against the powder blue walls. I kick off my sandals and hop up on her king sized bed. We've always watched TV via the comfort of her bed. During *The Wizard of Oz,* I'd huddle up under the comforter, any time the witch was on. She and I'd eat popcorn and talk about plants and recipes. I love our time together.

"Mr Gabe said he'd let Jersey use his frequent flyer miles to come visit over fall break. Would it be okay with you if she stayed here?"

"Of course, have you said anything to your mom?"

"Yeah, I said something to her before we went to dinner. Tell me, does my mom know about Tamers?"

"I don't think so, why?" She leaned over and flicked her DVR on to some dancing reality show she watches.

"No reason," I lied. "It's hard for me to believe she lived with my dad all of those years and never suspected anything. Not that she would guess that he is a Tamer, but you know…*something.*"

"I've thought about that before. Every family has secrets. Usually they have reasons behind their decisions not to say anything to the family. I honestly don't know. Tell me, how was your date with Caleb tonight?"

"It was fun, we didn't do much, but we always have fun together. You know that guy I told you Amber attacked in the lunchroom? She and I stopped to give him a ride to school this morning. Not only that, but she gave him *and* another guy a ride home. I hope it isn't another Erebus situation." I scooted to the edge of the bed. "I have some homework I need to finish before school. Good night, I love you." I leaned over and gave her a kiss on the cheek.

Before I start on my homework, I put on my "20 Minute Abs" DVD. If I'm wearing a slinky dress for the dance, I better get rid of my flab. Okay, maybe I don't have a lot of flab, but I'm not toned like I was when I played tennis. It takes a while but I finally start on my essay.

A tapping on my window sends me flying off my bed. It could be a Dark One. Do they knock before they drain your light? I run over to peek through the blinds…I gasp and cover mouth, holding back a scream. A face is on the other side.

"Thorne, what the hell?"

"Jessie, I need to talk to you." His brown eyes and beautiful face leave me with no other choice.

"Give me a minute; I'll meet you on the porch." I scramble to put on a bra and some clothes. What could he possibly want from me?

I tell grandma I'm going outside for a few minutes; she doesn't question me, which is good. Thankfully I don't have to come up with an excuse.

"Thorne, you know you could get shot, showing up at some girl's window in the middle of the night." His face is so serious; I feel stress vibrating from him in waves. "How did you know where I live? And more importantly, where my room is?"

He sticks his hands in his pockets and tilts his head back before talking. "Middle of the night? It's 10:00. Look, I know you don't know me, but I need you to trust me."

Conversations are never good when they start with trust me.
"Huh? Why should I trust you?"

"Can we sit?"

"Yeah, follow me, we'll go to the back porch. Be quiet, my mom fell asleep on the couch." Something about him was so enigmatic, yet he didn't send any bad vibes. He didn't make a sound as he followed me to the back porch. He reaches for the door and pulls it open for me. "Thank you," I whisper, as soon as we're outside. The lights on the patio are bright enough that I can see that he needs to shave.

"I know it's strange for me to show up like this. I need to talk to you."

"Okay, obviously, or you wouldn't be here."

He breaths in deeply, and exhales slowly. "Jessie, look, this is so out of protocol what I'm about to tell you. The powers that be have sent me. It wasn't my idea to reveal myself to you, but after the last couple of weeks, it's been decided that I must tell you who I am."

My heart is pounding so loud, I'm sure my shirt is moving with every beat. "Who you are? Please, don't tell me you're another Underworld escapee. Seriously don't tell me that. I will faint, right here, right now. I'll fall straight over. Me and the ground are like one these days. Spit it out."

"Don't faint, please don't do that. No...I'm not from the Underworld."

"Good, where are you from? Idaho?"

He looks at me quizzically. "Idaho? Why Idaho?"

"I don't know, I've never known anyone from Idaho. You're all mysterious, so I picked a random state. No worries."

"No, I'm not from Idaho. I know you've had to absorb a lot of information lately. I know that you recently found out about your gift, and I know that you've bonded with Caleb. I like him, which is good, since I'm going to be around more often. I also know who Mrs. Ward is…Fate. I'm your protector Jessie. I'm assigned to keep an eye on you. I've been following you since you arrived in New Bern."

I think I've stopped breathing, and the pain in my chest isn't anxiety, it is my impending death. One more crazy magical crap thing to put up with. Exactly what I wanted to learn about tonight. I was going to write my essay and curl up in my bed with Caleb's kiss on my mind. No, I can't have a normal night like that, no, I have to learn one more INSANE piece of my intricate puzzle. "So, you're stalking me? Are you some kind of creep?"

"No, Jessie, I'm not a creep. Stalker, maybe, but not a creep. I'm your protector, your own guardian."

"I don't even know you. I've never seen you before. I might be distracted lately, but I'd have recognized you. I don't."

"Listen, I'm not accustomed to revealing myself to my charge. The deal is, I'm your guardian, which means I'm guarding you against all the trouble you seem to find. I personally think you're in more harm from yourself than you are from Nyx."

The entire time he's talking, I'm asking myself if I've ever seen him before. "What does a guardian do?"

"Good question. First off, we're rarer than you Tamers are. We are assigned to various supernaturals for many different reasons. Some supers feel overwhelmed and go over the deep end, doing stupid things. It's frowned upon to hurt yourself, and we try to put a stop to it. As a guardian, I will appear to you in different forms. I can be as simple as a butterfly floating by, or as charming as an owl on its nightly hunt. A lot of foster children are supernaturals, sometimes I'm a foster child in a home to watch over them, and make sure they find the help they'll need. Some of the gifted aren't allowed to procreate with a human. They'll hide their pregnancy and then give the child up for adoption. Those children have a fifty fifty shot of inheriting their parent's gifts. Not that all gifted kids have powers that are good. Sometimes their powers need to be bound so they won't be a risk to themselves or anyone else. That is where I come in. I become a mentor to them, and I teach them how to protect themselves. I've never had a Tamer before; they usually don't have other Supers trying to find them. Their danger is from their counterparts, I think you call them Dark One. You on the other hand, are in danger from everything. As your guardian, I will put my life on the line for you. You're my only concern. I won't interfere in a battle that doesn't threaten you." He wipes the sweat off the bottle of water I gave him from the patio bar.

"You're telling me that you're a butterfly? Riiiiight."

"Hey, what's wrong with being a butterfly? No, I don't turn into a butterfly. I'm your guardian, not your fairy godmother."

Can someone tell me why my life is so damned confusing?
"Explain how you can protect me as a butterfly? While you're at it, can you explain how you're going to protect me at all? You're just going to be some voyeur that follows me?"

"Look Miss Skeptical, I'm doing what my superiors tell me to do. I have to keep you alive. Your destiny is too important to ignore. Sadly, you and your friends have become targets for the Underworld gods and goddesses. You couldn't upset something that Fate could help control, no, you upset the total psychos. Yes, you have a destiny and NO, I'm not telling you what it is."

"Is this like a North Carolina thing? Because when I lived in New York, the only crazy was my dad." I try to hide how annoyed he is making me. At this point, I'm not sure if I really care.

"Tomorrow, we'll talk about this more. Amber said you're riding with her in the morning, so I'll see you bright and early."

"You're just going to come in here, tell me you're my guardian angel and a butterfly and leave? How absurd is that!"

"Oh, honey, don't flatter yourself, I'm no angel. You think that's absurd, you'll love this next part...you can't tell anyone. Don't look at me like that. I'm sorry, but the rules are the rules. I know you and your friends like to bend the rules, but not this time. To assure that you won't tell anyone, there is a Dark One on stand-by to knock off your new BFF," he says cockily.

"You'll have my friend killed if I tell anyone? What the hell?"

He looks at me and cocks his head to the side. "It makes a difference doesn't it? It isn't a North Carolina thing either toots. This could have happened at any super school you went to. I have some homework to tend to. Be sure to arm the alarm when I leave, I don't want any bad guys to get you while you're sleeping."

Ugh, what a despicable ass. This is a guardian? "How am I supposed to keep this from Caleb? He hears my thoughts. Huh? You're going to kill my friend because I can't help thinking?"

"You ask a lot of questions. Don't worry about thinking it, somehow it's jumbled. I don't know how it works, but it isn't possible to spread the word via thoughts," he says as he stands up. "Good-night my little charge."

I try as hard as possible not to scream. Silently we walked through the house and without a word he left. I punch in the code to the alarm and head back to my room. My phone has only been on the charger for an hour, long enough to give Caleb a good-night call.

"Hey beautiful," Caleb says as he answers the phone.

I try to keep myself composed so he doesn't realize I'm on the verge of tears. "Hi you. I wanted to call and say good night."

"Is everything okay?"

No, everything isn't okay. "Yeah, I just wanted to hear your voice."

"Are you missing your dad?"

I do miss him, daily. "Yeah, a little. I can't really talk; I still have a little more homework to do. Good night." I close my eyes and envision him with me.

"Good night, I'll see you in the morning. I love you"

"Love you, too."

CHAPTER 11 KILLING AMBER

Amber's Jeep screeches its tires as we pull into the school parking lot. When we picked Thorne up, the jackass winked at me as he climbed into the back seat. After sitting up half the night trying to figure out what to do, I finally decided to go see Mrs. Ward first thing. After all, she is the one that seems to have made each obstacle for me. I told Amber to go on without me, and I'd see her in class.

As I lifted my hand to knock on her door, Mrs. Ward pulled it open.

"Good morning, Jessie. How are you enjoying your new school," she asked with a smile?

She motioned for me to sit down. "You know why I'm here. What I don't understand is why you trickle information to me."

"Trickle? Young lady, I assure you, I don't trickle. This isn't a ordinary little game we're playing. You're back on my radar, so something is going right. Thorne and I discussed it for hours;

before we decided you should know who he actually is. Your friend Amber, she is a loose cannon that girl. She is such a spurt of the moment person, it makes my job harder. She flits in and out of her path so much, it makes me dizzy."

"How on earth can you keep up with everyone in the world and their path?" It isn't a dumb question. "What do you mean about her in and out of her path? Is she teetering on being a Dark One?" I say, trying my best to keep my tone down and my temper in check.

"It's not for you to worry about. Your focus should solely be on your Light Tamer skills. Your path is changing, and I see a lot of good. I also see a dark time, despair, and fear. Your future depends on your strength."

"Where does Thorne fit into the picture? He said he is my guardian and if I tell anyone he'll kill Amber. What kind of guardian angel is that? He will *kill* her. It isn't like he will poke her with a needle, or whack her in the knee. He will kill her." I emphasize my words with my New York accent.

"He's a guardian, not an angel. He can't kill her. Killing an innocent is against the rules. He is just scaring you. He's so used to dealing with rogues and unloveables. I'll have a talk with him about his scare tactics. As for the rest, you're going to have to deal with him. With the Nyx situation hovering over us, especially now that she's been seen, we have to bump up security."

"Fine, I'll deal with it, but I'm telling Amber and Caleb about him."

She clucked her tongue and says, "No, you won't. I didn't say he can't relocate her to Alaska. I'm pretty sure the surfing is chilly there. You need to keep the secret. I'd suggest you figure out a way to deal with it." She looks down at her watch. "The bell is about to ring. Have a lovely day Miss Lucentee."

Nothing but a bunch of drama. *What fabulous piece of insanity will happen today?* .

The hallway is crowded as I weave my way through the accumulation of kids. I bump into a heavy-set guy, he's bigger than me, and he bumps me back, and I went flying into a clique of preppy girls. The kind that have hair extensions and carry designer backpacks, the kind that I'm not. One girl fusses and tells me to watch where I'm going. I scramble away from them before I do something stupid.

A tap on my right shoulder has me fall for the game boys' play, the one where I look right, and they are on my left. I turn expecting to see Caleb, to my chagrin, it's Thorne.

"I saw you leaving Mrs. Ward's office. How is the lovely Fate this morning?"

"I learned you can't kill my friends," I say with a smirk.

The first bell chimes through the halls. "Details, don't get hung-up on the small little wee details." He holds his fingers up an inch apart, to show me small. I'd like to snatch that smug look off of his face.

I feel hands on my waist from behind me, and instantly feel comforted. "Have fun in first hour beautiful."

I give him a quick peck on the lips. "You too. I have the paper signed for the weight lifting class. I didn't think she was going to agree to it, but she did and that's all that matters. See you in a bit." I say and Caleb turns to get to class before the tardy bell.

"Funny how things work out," Thorne says as he holds up his permission slip for the weight lifting class.

I growl and walk away to class.

Miss Raine escorted us to our secret classroom and then announced that she is staying with us. Mr James smiled and left to teach the other class, I guessed. Miss Raine pranced around the room in her tie-dyed sun dress talking about the changes in the weather will affect our ability to pull light to us. Watch the weather. Keep your eye on the barometric pressure. Do this, do that, it was all overload.

"Are you paying attention Miss Lucentee?"

No. "Uh, well, not exactly," I say, voice shaky with nerves.

"As I was saying class, our fall break will be in September. The fall equinox happens that weekend. Now you're aware of Tamers, your body and instincts will go into hyper-mode. You'll be able to spot other Tamers, and some of you will have the ability to spot small children that are a Tamer too. Anything to do with spells, incantations, fire, earth, spirit, will be easy to retain. It will be the beginning of our daylight hours being shortened. Obviously, Tamers are able to get through winter months with little complications. You might find this interesting. During the shortened days, the Dark Ones do a semi-hibernation through winter. It's obvious that they survive and thrive from the light. It's hypothesized that like a squirrel they store up during the warmer, brighter months. Not that you'll be altogether safe, so you should always carry your flashlights. Everyone has been given their flashlight holsters. Carry them in your backpacks, and keep a flashlight in your locker. Batteries are free to you for your flashlights; you can stop by the secretary's office before and after school to stock up."

I feel a slight buzz from my pocket. I discreetly pull it out to see who texted me. Amber of course.

Amber: Did you smell his cologne??? Deee Lightful!

Me: No

Amber: Your sniffer must be broken.

Me: I guess

Yes, I smelled his cologne. He smells like Jimmy Johnson from my old school. I wasn't about to tell her that, or she'd have a cow.

"Miss Lucentee, is your lap talking to you?" Miss Raine asks. She tucks a piece of hair behind her ear, and I notice her tattoo on her wrist is glowing.

"My lap is fine, I was checking if I had some change for the soda machine. I'm sorry."

From the corner of my eye, I see Thorne shake his head.

"Do you have something to say Mr Woodson?"

"Yes ma'am," Thorne replies. "I do have a question. When did you find out about Light Tamers, if you're not one?"

She tilts her head to the side, as though she is carefully deciding what she would say. "A darned good question. We'll be going into this in the next segment of this class, but I'll tell you a little about it. I'm a member of a branch that is affiliated with the Rosicrucian Order. It is a society for the spiritually gifted. My gifts are also of the healing kind, and my chapter of the Order is extremely small. There are about fifty of us throughout the world. I've always known about Light Tamers, there's never been a time I didn't. My father was highly involved with the Order, so I grew up with it around me. Your chapter is much larger, but, not the largest group. My father and the head of the Tamers charter are close friends. We had family vacations and we trained together, that is how I know about you." Someone asked if she is a witch. "Ah, no, I'm not a witch. Our group doesn't have a fancy name. We're just known as the healer. My gift as a healer is purely physical. I heal wounds and sometimes I can heal an illness."

Carmen raises her hand. "If you're able to heal, why do you need the potions?"

"Sometimes you need a healing unguent, or a potion to help speed things up. My power can be drained very quickly; I'm not God, I can't heal everyone. You'll understand this even more as you become a healer. Okay, on to more information about the equinox weekend. We'll be having a dance for juniors and seniors on that Saturday. It will be held downtown at the convention center. There are sign-up sheets for decorating committee and chaperones in the main office. Please don't pass up this time, you're not too cool to join in the fun. You'll only be teens for a few more years, enjoy it while you can. There will be extra credit for those students that help out. Okay, on to another exciting thing. Next week we will have a guest speaker. Her name is Chrissy, and she is an animal healer, she can speak to animals too. She and I've been in training all summer, and I'm excited for all of you to hear her story."

I wonder if Caleb would be interested in helping out. I can only imagine the four letter words Amber will say when I ask her. Oh, that's right, she isn't saying them, she's making up words to use in place of the super bad words. When I asked her to take weight lifting class with me; she almost fell over laughing.

"…respect the earth. We're not endorsing witchcraft, we're endorsing the love and energy the earth, sun, and moon provide us. In alchemy we will use such things as crystals, essential oils and items you can probably find in your own cupboards. These items will serve as a catalyst for you to heal. Many of you in this classroom will be a doctor of some sort." A spurt of laughter broke the lecture up for a second. "Two out of three Tamers *will* go forth as a doctor. There are all types of doctors. A doctorate can be given to scholars, physicians, engineers. Your positive energy is needed in all of those fields. The other *one* Tamer will usually be a stay at home healer." Miss Raine went over to a cabinet and pulled out what looks like a tissue box from where I was sitting. She handed the box to Carmen, telling her to take a crystal and pass it on."

Amber turns around to me. "You have to be kidding me, we're going to play with rocks? I think she's got a few rocks loose in her head, if you know what I mean."

"Crystal's are thought to have the strongest healing powers from the earth," Thorne says. We all turn around to face him as he speaks.

"Oh, no, I didn't mean anything derogatory about it. She's just so intense," Amber says timidly (totally out of character for her).

The box of crystals made it to our end of the room. The one I pick is small and jagged but clear and pretty. The stone feels cold as ice in the palm of my head.

"Can anyone tell me what the metaphysical aspect of a quartz crystal is?" Miss Raine asks and opened up a small notebook and wrote something in it.

Carmen is the only one that raises her hand. "Crystals amplify the mind, body and spirit. They will absorb energy from the earth, moon and sun. I know when my grandma's arthritis is acting up, she says her crystals help the pain. Before anyone gets the gumption to say she is a witch, I'd highly suggest you keep your thoughts to yourself."

At the end of class, we each have a quartz crystal and an amethyst cluster, which is said to help calm the spirit. Miss Raine said that it helps with attention deficit disorder, and if we keep one in our pocket it will help us focus. The bell rang, I barely made it to the door and Caleb is standing there waiting for me. He hands me a folded up piece of paper, and he tells me not to open it until I'm alone.

Rob and Caitlyn are already at our pod when I sit down. Rob is holding up a Hello Kitty mirror and checking his teeth, and Caitlyn is doodling as usual.

"So, tell me. Are you and Caleb in love? Please tell me you are," Rob asks dramatically.

I pull out a spiral notebook and slip my note inside so I can read it when things settle down in class. Rob is leaning across his desk waiting for me to answer his question. "You don't beat around the bush do you?"

"No, so tell me…are you?"

One beat, two beats, three beats…breathe in, breathe out. "I think so." I say, but inwardly I wish he'd leave me alone.

"He has perfect lips, I bet he kisses wonderfully." He looks at me for a moment, before his attention is taken to the front of the class.

Mrs. Jones starts tapping her foot in annoyance. "As you can see on the work table, I have 32 copies of The Innocent Man. I want everyone to come up and take one. Silently, I want you to read the first three chapters. When you have finished, I want you to return the book and then I want you to write down how you *feel* about the story. Two pages, single spaced. When you're done, come up and get the book and continue reading."

Someone asks why we can't keep the book; instead of returning it and going back to get it again.

"This is an exercise on how well you remember the characters, the plot, and the way you felt as you read it. I don't want anyone to thumb through the book to remember, I want you to work from your gut. Our life is filled with people telling us stories; it will be up to us, what we remember, how we felt, and if it's truth or fiction." Looking around the room, she smiles. "Has anyone in here read anything by Mr John Grisham before?"

He's one of my favorite authors, and I've read all of his books, including this one. I don't raise my hand, in my attempt at blending in. No one admits to reading his books.

Rob wouldn't shut up so I never had a chance to take a look at my note.

CHAPTER 12 ~ JEALOUSLY IS UGLY

For once, I'm in the hallway waiting on Caleb. I stood outside of his classroom and can barely see him, but I finally do. He is there, and a girl with bright green barrettes and curly red hair is talking to him. She keeps touching his arm and throwing her head back in laughter as if he's the funniest person on earth. My teeth clench and my blood feels like it's on fire. I've never experienced anything like this...jealousy. I'm seriously jealous of some girl because she is paying attention to my boyfriend. Get a grip, I tell myself.

Caleb looks up and sees I'm standing in the hallway. She follows his gaze and gives me a fake smile. They say a quick goodbye and he comes over to walk with me to the cafeteria. "Hey beautiful, how was class?"

I try to pretend it didn't bother me, but it did. I hated her hand on him, and I hated the way she laughed. I hated that he didn't tell her to stop touching him. I hate the way I feel.

"What was all of that about?" My eyes meet his, and he knows I'm jealous.

"That was nothing, trust me, you ready for lunch," he asks.

"Why was she touching you? It isn't like she can't keep her hands to herself." I feel the New Yorker in me rearing its ugly head. "Why didn't you stop her?"

"Jessie, you're being stupid."

I refuse to take his hand as we walked towards the cafeteria. "Stupid? You think I'm being stupid? You can't answer a simple question, and you're calling *me* stupid. You can eat lunch alone." I storm off to get in line.

"Women!" I hear Caleb say loud enough for me to hear him.

Amber runs over and grabs a tray, getting in line behind me. "Where's Caleb?"

"I don't know, and right now, I don't care." I grab a slice of lemon cream pie and a sweet tea as I slide my tray to the register.

"You're going to have some type of sugar induced coma if you eat all of that. Suicide by lemon pie is a sticky way to go." She grabs a chocolate brownie and some chocolate milk. "Mine has milk, that's healthy. Why are you mad at Mr Charming?"

"I don't know. Some girl kept touching him, and he didn't try to brush her off or anything. My mom would say I have the green eye monster in me."

We walk to the table we've sat at all week. Thorne is sitting there with a bag from a fast food restaurant and eating fries.

"Hello ladies," Thorne says.

Amber practically throws her food on the table and nonchalantly scooted her chair closer to him. "Hey…Miss Perfect is fuming over a fight with Caleb."

"I'm not fuming, I'm just a little pissed off."

"Sorry, she isn't fuming…pissed off is a totally different category." Amber shoves a massive bite of brownie in her mouth.

"This girl had her paws all over him, and he didn't do anything about it. I know that sounds dumb, but there was something about the way she looked at him."

"Yeah, that is dumb. Was he pawing back? Did he act like he has something to hide? Or did you forget to wear your big girl panties today?" Thorne asks. Amber practically shot chocolate milk out of her nose as she choked on what he said.

"Whatever." I know they're right. We've never had a fight before, what if he breaks up with me? What if he decides it would be better being with another girl and just being friends with me?

"Where's the tramp at? Do you know who it was?" Amber asks as she looks around the room.

"I don't know her name. I've never seen her before. Her hair is red and curly, she has green barrettes holding it back. Before you ask, yes she's pretty. Not as much pretty as she is cute. She'd probably look better without her braces.

Amber clamps her hand to her mouth and moans out an "ohhhhhh."

"Do you know who it is? What does ohhhhhh mean?"

Thorne shrugs his shoulders. "I'm new here; I don't know any of the girls other than you two."

"It sounds like Meredith, you better hope not. She's a hoe like no hoe you know."

"What do you mean hoe?"

"Don't tell me you didn't have hoes in your old school. She likes sex, she tells everyone who will listen, about her desire to sleep with every guy in our class. Guys love her, why wouldn't they…"

I stop her before she had a chance to finish the sentence. "I'm not worried about *that*, Caleb wouldn't go mess around with anyone."

Thorne laughs out loud. "He's not a saint. Any guy that has it flung in his face non-stop is bound to give in eventually."

"Caleb isn't like that, he's a good guy."

"Caleb might be a good guy, but he's not blind. I'm just sayin' you shouldn't push him away. You might be pushing him into the wrong hands." Thorne said skeptically. "I'd find out more about this girl and figure out what her motive is. If her quest is the entire class, he might just be a notch in her bedpost."

"Ewwww, that's horrible Thorne."

"Are you listening to me? He isn't that way," I said.

Thorne set his cup of tea down on the table and leaned back in his chair. "I didn't think he woud, I was trying to make you think about what kind of guy he is. Give him a break. As a matter of fact, here's your chance."

Caleb approaches the table, and I see the hurt on his face. "I'm sorry, that was dumb of me." I say trying my best not to show how pathetic I feel.

He pulls me in and kisses my forehead. "Are you okay? You seemed really on edge earlier."

I let out the breath I'd been holding. "I'm fine. I feel terrible you didn't sit with us for lunch."

"It wasn't that bad. I had a chance to sit with Brad and Michael, they're twins and don't have many friends here at the school."

Amber shoots me a thumbs up.

"I need to turn in my permission slip. Can we go see the weight lifting coach?"

Caleb shakes his head yes, and we turn to leave when we hear Thorne.

"Hey, slow up, I need to turn in my slip too."

"He's taking weight lifting?" Caleb whispers to me, I whisper yes back to him.

A chair squeals across the floor behind us. "Oh for cripes sake, I guess I'm going to take weight lifting too. I feel so damned left out. If I get hurt, it's all on you!"

Caleb and I laugh as Amber joins us in the hallway.

"Some kids had asked me when we'll be getting together again to practice what we did at my house. I was thinking tomorrow night would be good. I sent a text to my dad, and he said it was OK with him. He's going to text your grandma and have her to come over and help. We can go see a late movie when everyone leaves."

"I think that would be perfect."

"What's going on? Are you having a party or something?" Thorne smiles and smoothes chapstick on his lips.

I avoid his gaze, knowing that if I don't, I'll blush and give away our secret. I can not imagine Amber liking Alaska.

Caleb gave him a short overview of what happened at his house two weeks ago. We all agreed that it would be beneficial to have a refresher, and now that we know more Tamers, we can have more people show up.

"Let's give the lovebirds a few minutes alone, they're practically conjoined twins." Amber waved as she happily walked away with Thorne.

The coach for the Weight Lifting class wasn't there, but we all left our permission slips in the clear box on the door.

"C'mere," Caleb pushed on the door, and it opened to the weight room. He pulled on my hand and I followed him into the locker room. The smell of sweat and the sound of water trickling from the showers gave it the Stephen King bogeyman feel. Across the room was another door. "I want to show you something." I giggled as we ran through the room; my reaction is to laugh when I'm scared. The door opened easily, the smell of chlorine practically knocked me off my feet.

"Wow, a pool? I didn't know we had a swim team."

"I don't think we do, that's what's strange. They use the pool for scuba diving lessons and survival skills. Look how deep it is. I've never seen a pool that deep before. There isn't a shallow end either."

We stopped for a second, and he turned me to face him. "Jess, why were you so mad?"

Because some crazed hoe was trying to make moves on my man. "I don't know, instinct I guess." *Because she's pretty and has that cute bouncy red hair. Ugh!*

He drapes his arms over my shoulders and puts his forehead to mine. "You're all that matters to me, you're the most significant reason for my life. This is for real, not something I'd screw things up to be with the school hoe."

I laugh nervously. "So you know she's a hoe?"

"I know, but not first hand or anything." He pulls me into a hug. "Jess, when I said I love you...I meant it."

Before I can respond, his lips are on mine. Chlorine wafted all around us, but we were somewhere else. We were in our reality. His tongue, silky smooth in my mouth. My heart is beating faster than a marathon runner. His hands, strong and gentle, stroking my lower back. A moan escapes my throat, I pull back and look into his eyes, and I see my reflection. He leans in and kisses my neck, and I melt into him. The memory exchange from him to me...was him seeing me in my school uniform. He'd felt happy and proud that I'm his girlfriend. He has access to most of my memories, we don't know why I only receive his memories when we kiss. Sometimes it would be of him and his mom and sometimes it was things like picking out underwear to wear for the day. I've never shared that bit of trivia with him.

"Eh, hem. Students aren't allowed in here without a teacher. The way you two are pawing at each other, I'm making a logical guess you're unsupervised. You should be ashamed of yourselves, practically making a baby at school. That's what's wrong with kids today, they think it won't happen to them. Before you know it, you'll be a statistic and be an unwed mother. You need to think with your brains."

"Thank you for the pep talk, we'll leave. Sorry to disturb your work day. Just for your information, I know two teenaged moms, and they are devoted parents and exceptional students. Just because some people make the wrong decision doesn't mean they've ruined their life. I'd never make that decision, but you're acting as if they're serial killers, and they're not." I tug on Caleb's hand. "Let's go, we'll be late."

We run to the locker room, the guy is yelling behind us that we're going to slip and fall. "That must be the maintenance man that everyone was talking about last year. His wife went off the deep end and stabbed the neighbor in the front yard. She is in the loony bin, and he takes his frustrations out on the students."

"As long as he doesn't know who we are and doesn't report us, he can be grumpy."

CHAPTER 13. GRANDMA

"Jessie! Come on, we're going to the Wal Marts for refreshments for your friends."

Grandma is standing in the living room with her Seven jeans, red stilettos, and red v-neck t-shirt, not a man on this planet would call her grandma. She may not resemble a grandma, and she might even be sexy, but she is all grandma on the inside.

"Stilettos for Wal Mart? Are you trolling for a husband?" I snag my purse, and we head out to her BMW. She bought a SUV last month, but she said it makes her feel old. The bad thing about taking her car is the size. We can only pack a few bags in the trunk of her two-seater.

"Do you honestly believe I'd run off with someone I met in a discount store?" We both broke out in laughter.

"Not really. Have you ever thought of Mr Gabe? He's pretty good looking, for a dad."

"Really? I haven't noticed...okay, so what if I did? I don't think he'd want to go out with an old fool like me."

"You're not old, and he isn't a kid. He's in his late forties, and you're in your mid fifties. It takes a ten year span to call you a cougar."

"You're sweet. He's still mourning the loss of his wife. I remember what I was like when your grandpa died. It took me years before I could even talk about him."

I lean over and change the station. "I get it. I wouldn't rule him out though. You two have a lot of fun when you're together. Both of you know what it's like to lose someone you love so much."

The drive is approximately five minutes away, depending on the stop light pattern. Grandma is known for her lead foot and cheeky mouth. I love her the way she is, because she isn't like everyone else. We made it in four minutes flat.

We're barely in the store and here comes Thorne from the nutrition isle. "Hey Jess, fancy meeting you in such a common place."

Grandma nudges me, "Who's the hot tamale?"

"I'll tell you in a bit." I study Thorne's face for some sign he was here for himself and not stalking me. "Thorne, this is my grand….Miss Gayle. What are you getting on the nutrition isle?"

"I figure if we're gonna take the weight lifting class, I might as well bulk up. They carry the protein powder; it'll make me get some guns like you're boyfriend."

Grandma takes the cart and heads over to the produce section.

"Did you follow me here?"

"I suppose I did." He smiles and runs his hand through his hair. "Although, I beat you into the store."

I bet his hair is soft and full. Aghhhhh! I did not just think that! "The bad guys are searching for me in here? Give me a break."

"They're searching for your kind everywhere. When they find out New Bern is crawling with them, all of you will be in danger. You have me, who do they have?"

I turn and head to electronics. I've been thinking about getting another e-reader, or possibly a tablet. My sixteenth birthday is coming up next week, and I'm sure I'll get some money from my dad. He hasn't called me all week. I hope he's okay. I'm probably the only kid my age who doesn't want a car. I'm afraid of being responsible for other people. My nerves get the better of me when I'm behind the wheel. My palms sweat, my heart pounds, my legs shake and I hyperventilate before I ever pull out of the parking spot. I'll leave the driving to the people that can handle the inner chaos.

"Tell me, what exactly will you do? I mean, do you shoot them or stab them? Won't you go to prison for killing someone?"

He leans in, I feel his breath on my ear, and he whispers to me, "I have a big sword."

"You're going to walk into school wielding a sword? Yeah, even Fate can't get you past school security."

"Want me to tell you a secret? I have it with me." He raises his eyebrows at me, so damn cute and so damn aggravating.

"You're carrying an invisible sword? Okay, I've taken in a lot of crazy lately, but I'm not that gullible."

Thorne pats me on the shoulder. "Sweets, you haven't seen crazy yet. If I have to pull this thing out, it means the shit has hit the fan. I have the Fragarach, the sword of retaliation. One swipe and it sends flames burning its victim until life escapes them. The only thing that can heal them is the hands of healing."

"Why would you cut someone that you'd want healed?"

"You're not experienced in sword fights are you? Sometimes the innocent get in the way." He cocks his head to the side. "Your grandma is ready to leave, she's by the bananas."

"Good-bye Thorne."

"Hasta la vista."

She may have been in the banana section at one time, but she had darted halfway across the store with lightning speed. I found her near the unmentionables.

"How do you feel about thongs? I spend all day trying not to get a wedgie, what's the point of a string up your bum?" Grandma holds up a hot pink thong.

"It's so you don't have panty lines." I pick up a pack of thongs in wild colors. "Here, you can get a variety pack."

"Why not go commando if you want to keep the panty lines at bay?"

"Eww, that's gross."

She shakes her head back and forth. "You're grossed out by commando and not butt floss? I hope you don't get into any accidents and, the hospital has to cut you out of your clothes. Your hiney will be exposed to the paramedics."

"If I'm in an accident and they're cutting me out of my clothes, I'm guessing being embarrassed is not going to be an issue."

Grandma grabs the thongs and tosses them in the cart. We rounded the corner to look at the bras, my least liked section.

Grandma dangles a white generic bra. "You think they have one of those ladies who come and measure your boobies? I'm not sure what size I am these days."

"Shhhh, no I don't think they have anyone here to measure you."

Without warning grandma is pulling the bra from the plastic hanger and putting it on over her clothes.

"Grandma, what on earth are you doing?" I put my hand to my forehead and say a silent prayer Thorne isn't lurking around the corner. "They have dressing rooms."

She isn't paying any attention to me. She's got the bra on over her red t-shirt and looks undoubtably crazy. "Where's a mirror, I need to see what I look like."

"Bonkers, you don't need a mirror to prove it either. Okay, the show is over, please take it off." In my attempt at being discreet I begin walking slowly to the socks.

"You're no fun. I figured you'd find it fun to try on the boobie slings. I mean, for goodness sake, you have some serious knockers."

I'm shocked she said that out loud. "Oh, I'm not calling you Miss Gayle in front of anyone for an entire year. Leave my boobs out of this," I huff. Between being mortified and finding it a little funny, I refrain from cracking a smile. I think of a payback, and it suddenly hits me. "Grandma! Do we need to get you those Depends so you stop leaking?" I say loud enough for anyone to hear.

"Playing dirty are you?" Grandma says and busts out laughing. "Let's get outta here. I'm hungry for a Gyro and sweet tea. How about Famous? You can get a sub or some pasta."

"I'm down with that. Can Amber go with us? The anniversary of her brother's death is this weekend. I'm sure it has been on her mind. Her sister and parents started family counseling, but she refuses to go. She said she'd rather go alone, but she doesn't want her parents to pay an extra co-pay for her. Did I tell you her dad won't let her get a job? I think the vibe in her house is heavy."

"I forgot about her brother. Of course, send her a message and tell her we will be at her house in twenty minutes. It's essential for you to listen to her if she needs to talk. Let's drop this stuff at home and go get her. You know you have to ride in the granny mobile." That's what we call her Escalade.

20 MINUTES LATER

The Escalade glided over the dirt road to Amber's house. The house is a Cape Cod style home, and it looks like a magazine cover. The only difference is the secret ramp on the side of the giant porch. Her father is paralyzed from the waist down from a surfing accident last summer. The same one that took her brother's life.

I knock on the door and Delores the caregiver answers. "Hi Jessie, I'm taking dinner out of the oven, so you'll have to excuse me." She scurries off towards the kitchen.

Amber's dad wheels into the room. "Hi Jessie, how have you been? Are you feeling okay? Amber told me that you were pretty sick."

"Thank you, no, I'm fine."

"Oh, look who's here, Miss Perfect. Thank you for honoring us with your presence," Jasmine, Amber's little sister hatefully says.

"Jasmine Lee, get to your room!" He turns his chair to face me again. "I'm sorry, Lee's having a tough time this week. We all are if truth be told. Amb will be down in a minute, would you like some tea?"

"No thank you. My grandma is in the car, I'll let her know it will be a few minutes." He typically stayed in the study every time I'd been over to the house.

"Beeeeeeeee, I've been dying to go to Famous. Have you had their baklava?" Amber turns to her dad. "I'll be home later. Mom is at bookclub, and the little house of horror reject is up in her room having a tantrum." She makes a feeble attempt at putting her arm over my shoulder. My 5'9 to her 5'1 make us a pretty odd couple.

"Hold up, let me see!" I demand, and she gives me a quick smile and does a pirouette, then curtsied. Her green and black striped knee-highs match the black and green polka dot platforms she has on. Her little black skirt has black and pink bows all along the hem. I'd never be able to pull off the off the shoulder tee, a neon tank top like her. Amber is addicted to changing her hair color and wearing. Today isn't any different. "Blue extensions?"

"Electric blue, do you love it? I love love love them. Some of the blue hair on top is my hair." To be festive, she wore long eyelashes with one single swallow tail blue feather. "Do you love my eye make-up? I found a tutorial on Youtube to do the glam punk look."

"Totally. I totally love it...on you. Grandma is going to faint, she's in the car waiting."

My favorite part about the restaurant is the authentic food. All the way there, Amber chattered about the ridiculous notion that Nyx would bother with her. The one valid point was the only thing they did was kiss, why would a thousand year old relationship have friction now. I tend to agree with her, it is ridiculous.

After taking a seat in a semi-circle booth, we placed our order with a bouncy happy waitress. A group of police officers are right next to us, and a young family are in the booth behind us. When we're in public, we try to keep the Tamer talk to a minimum. It wouldn't be good for cops to overhear us talking about banishing gods to the Underworld.

"Miss Gayle, do you ever date?" Amber asked.

I sigh, thinking about our earlier conversation about Mr Gabe.

"Is this a conspiracy? You two aren't planning on playing match maker are you? Believe me when I say, I don't blind date. As for your question Amber, yes, I've had a date or two with some mighty nice men."

"Do tell," Amber says.

I can tell grandma is thinking about the way she is going to answer nosey Amber.

"Well, I went out with one fool man that runs a local company. He only wanted one thing, and you know what that is."

Sheesh, if she starts talking about her sex life, I'm going to run out of here screaming.

"He was just looking for a booty-call? How old was he?" Amber asked.

"Booty-call, what on earth is that?"

"You know, bow-chica-wow-wow." She said as danced in her seat.

"Amber, you did not just go there!" I say with my mouth full of gyro meat trying to hide my rudeness with my hand.

"Oh, I went there."

Grandma Gayle laughed at the two of us. "He wanted my money, dirty minded little girl."

"Who me?" Amber asked and played shy. "Okay, who else?"

Grandma glances at me, before she answers the question. "Don't turn around, but I dated one of the men at that table. It's a small town, not a lot to pick from."

Both of us practically broke our necks as we snapped them towards the cop filled table.

"Ewww, was it the old one with the jar head hair cut?" I whisper. Grandma smiles mischievously.

"Was it the blonde?" Amber asks.

"Nope, both of you're wrong. See the guy at the end of the table? He has that fifties movie star look."

"What? The guy that looks like he's twenty-five?" He's handsome and young, dark hair and light-colored eyes. I couldn't tell what color they are from my vantage point though. I think he looks like Tatum Channing, I'm not familiar with too many fifties hunks.

She smiled smugly at us. "He is not in his twenties. I know this, because we met at his thirtieth birthday party at the Woods Country Club."

"Now *that's* a cougar. Me ow," Amber whispers loudly.

"He's easy on the eyes, but not much of a conversationalist. Too bad. He comes from a wealthy family."

I check around the room for our waitress and wouldn't you

know…Thorne is at a table alone. I thought I saw someone at the table when we arrived; the customer had the menu up covering his face. He must feel me staring at him, he looks up and winks at me. *He is inescapable.*

A minute later, I have Amber grabbing my wrist, digging her nails in with her excitement. "He's here."

Knowing exactly who she's talking about, I play dumb. "Who?"

"Thorne…he's over there. He looks hot, don't you think. No, of course you don't. Agh, did you see him? He saw me talking about him. He is too delicious for this town. He makes me want to slap someone," Amber rambles uncontrollably.

"I've no idea what you're talking about. You want to randomly hit people because you think he's cute? I'm so confused."

She smacks her hands on the table and yelps like a dog with rabies. "You'll survive. I'm inviting him to sit with us. You don't mind do you Miss Gayle?" She holds her hands up in prayer.

Grandma looks at her like she has lost her marbles all over the floor. "Go," she says.

"I'm gonna do it," she says and gets up from the table.

He walks over and sits down. Of course he does. I wish Caleb was here. If I concentrate real hard, I can send him a direct message. That's a perk to having our bond. The good part is we can talk secretly, the bad part, he can hear my thoughts when we're together. I've been practicing keeping him out of my head. When he first told me about us being Light Tamers, he told me he has my memories too. At first, I was only able to hear him when we kissed. If he concentrates, we can communicate. It can be embarrassing when you know that he knows every single thing about you. That's why I can't understand how I'll keep Thorne from showing up in my memories. I still only get Caleb's memories when we kiss.

"Jess, are you with us?" Amber shakes my arm to get my attention.

I move closer to grandma as Amber and Thorne scooted in.

"Miss Gayle, this is Thorne. Thorne, this is Miss Gayle, Jessie's mother's mother."

"It's a pleasure to meet you Thorne. I heard you had an eventful first day at Parca Academy."

"Yes, it was. I've never had a girl throw herself at me."

"I did not *throw myself* at you. I simply marked my territory."

What are you a dog? "You didn't just say that?" I shake my head.

She tucks her blue extension behind her ear and flashes her best innocent smile. "Clearly it was the most dramatic thing I could come up with. I can't help it if I'm a trend setter."

Grandma chokes on her coffee. "My goodness, someone is feisty tonight. Anyone up for milk with your baklava?"

I'm sure if he sticks around, Amber will make sure to keep him entertained. I wonder how it works, if he's a guardian, can he date a Tamer? It would suck if he was in the middle of making out with Amber, and his guardian bell goes off. Talk about awkward moments.

"What school did you come from?"

"Yeah, where did you come from?" Amber repeats.

"I'm from Idaho, it was a small town with a smaller school." Thorne says, using the Idaho comment I gave him the other night.

"You're the boy that was talking to Jessie at the Wal Marts aren't you?"

Thorne flashes her a big toothy grin. "Yes ma'am, I was there picking up a few things. Amber, if you're not staying over with Jessie, I'll give you a ride home. I owe you a ride."

What's he up to? I can practically feel Amber willing her thoughts to me.

Amber audibly swallows, her feather on her eyelash is giving away her trembling. "That's cool. Did you get a car?"

"It's my uncle's; he said I could use it at night."

Grandma and I share a knowing look. Amber the snarky teenage girl is getting soft on us.

CHAPTER 14. RAINE

I rode home from school with Caleb to his house. We stopped at a bakery and picked up a gazzilion cupcakes that we'd ordered the day before. Grandma and Mr Gabe were already getting things ready for tonight. The first week is finally over, and hopefully I wouldn't meet any other supernatural being. Be careful what you wish for, or so I'm told.

 Amber had been on cloud nine all day. Somehow she convinced Thorne that her paralyzed dad was going to work on her Jeep tonight. My suspicion of him is the broken heart he will leave her with. What's the point of wasting time with someone you're not bonded with? Amber told me she doesn't have to be boyfriendless to find her bonded person. My thoughts are it is an excuse to be where I'm at, without causing suspicion.

A person I didn't expect to see is Miss Raine. She's with Mr Gabe setting out a veggie tray and ranch dressing. Everyone knows everything is better with ranch dressing.

"Hi Miss Raine, I didn't know you'd be here."

"This is a excellent opportunity for me to teach you the ways of the Light Tamer, without a bunch of rules around the way I teach it. You'll learn more in two hours tonight, then you've learned in one week at the school. Mrs. Ward is a warden of the rules, and it is her way or the highway. Those same rules do not apply to us in a meeting outside of the school. Would you mind helping me set up a table in the den?" She took a breath and smiled at me. In her special way, she is more relaxed, and that is being generous. Okay, maybe she isn't as uptight as she usually is. She still made me nervous though.

I'm helping Miss Raine set up a table. Amber sent a text that she is picking up some chicken nuggets from Filet of Chicken. Do you need her to pick up anything? I thought to Caleb.

Is she wound tight?

No, not as severe as she is at school. I love you, I can't wait to have some alone time.

Ah, I love you too beautiful. Alone time, hmmm, you, me and moonlight bouncing off the river. If you could see the images in my head, you might run out of here screaming.

I felt heat rushing to my face as I tried to figure out what his imagination was doing. I look up, taking note that Miss Raine is looking at me like I have six eyes. *Rats! I gotta go, she can tell I'm talking to you.* "I found a white tablecloth for the table."

"That should work." She looked away from me, as if she knew she interrupted a private moment between Caleb and I.

We loaded the table with the goodies from the bakery and plastic ware. Her decorating skills on a table for teenagers is pretty awesome. Just about the time we finished she asked if I'd go sit and talk with her for a few minutes. *No, you kinda freak me out.* "Yeah, of course," I said and smiled sweetly. I asked Mr Gabe if we could borrow the FROG for a few minutes to have a one on one with Miss Raine. Sadly, he said yes.

"I make you a little nervous don't I? You have nothing to worry about Jessie, we're on the same side. The fact that you're an original Tamer is incredible. The odds of us having one in our own backyard, is about seven million to one."

"If I'm the last one, wouldn't it be greater odds? If we're going to put numbers with it, shouldn't we make it accurate?"

"Regardless of the number, I'm thrilled you're here. I'm worried that your training is lagging a little. You're much more advanced at your skill then you realize. Your aura glows with power."

"It does? Did Mrs. Ward show you one of her aura photos of me or something?" She shook her head no. "How *do* you know all of this?"

"It's part of what I do. I'm a variation of your species, and I'm gifted with special healing powers."

Species, really? Like we're zoo animals. She rubs me the wrong way. I wonder if there are any teachers at the school that are just normal people. The kind that assigns homework and wears therapeutic shoes.

Miss Raine smiled, and a calm rushed over me. "Jessie, can you feel that the atmosphere changed in here?"

I shrug my shoulders. "I guess. Did you do something to calm my nerves?" *Like valium my butt so you can do some hocus pocus magic.*

A smile lit up her face. "Very good, yes I did. I want to show you how to calm a room. You'll find it easier, if you're calm yourself. If you're put into a compromising situation, use this ability. It's one of those skills that get better with practice."

"Not that I'm trying to rush you or anything, but the company will be here in two hours." *Drama much?*

She turns to look at me, her hands clasped together. Her aura blends with the light that spewed from the window behind her. Something inside me tells me to trust her, but I can tell she's going to hold out on me. I'm a kid, everything is on a need-to-know basis. "Come closer."

I stand to walk over to her, my shoe catches and I stumble. I stop in front of her feeling a little gawky and a lot nervous.

"Jessie, put your hands straight out in front of you." I did as I was told. "Now, close your eyes and concentrate on the light in the room. Imagine the light being pulled into you. Keep calm and harness your ability."

I ruminate about the light and my hands start to warm up. I opened my eyes, and to my dismay, a ball of light is resting in the palms of my hand.

"Beautiful isn't it?"

"I did this by thinking? How incredible. What do I do with it?" I locked eyes with her, and I suddenly felt her smile. Not just see it, I feel it. "Woa, what happened?"

"You tapped into my essence."

"Oh crap, I'm sorry. I didn't take any light from you did I?"

"No, I'm not a Light Tamer, I'm a healer. We're totally different. If I'd been a Tamer, it still wouldn't be anything to worry about. Tapping into the essence is another way of connecting with the subject. You can tap into anyone, if you lock eyes with them. The down side is they can tap into you too. Typically it won't be anything to worry about."

"Typically, isn't a word that describes my life right now."

"True, before you lose your concentration, I want you to push the light ball into me."

"How?"

"Here, I'll hold my hand out. Now take the light and hold your hand under mine, and then push up until we are holding hands."

As our hands touched, the light flowed from my fingers into hers. "Incredible! What just happened?"

"That, is your healing power. Yours is strong. Have you been light headed and faint frequently?"

So there is a reason for all of the fainting lately. "Yes, I have. Is that bad?"

"Because you're so powerful, you're drawing light from everywhere. The buildup needs to be released. You need to heal something or someone. You can touch a person and heal their broken heart, or if someone is in a cast you can heal their bone. You can touch strangers to release some light, it will keep you from becoming over stimulated with power." She pauses for a second before continuing her talk. "The possibilities are endless. You need to harness your light and begin healing with it. This is astounding news. We'll have to hide you when you graduate. They will hunt you like a fatty at an all you can eat food bar fighting for the last dinner roll." (Holy cannoli she just made a joke.) "Your life will never be the same. Caleb is a bonus; the two of you will do extraordinary things. It's fascinating your dad didn't try to take your light. Not that I think he would do it to be bad, please don't get me wrong. He and I used to be friends before you were born. Lydia and I were friends too. She was fun to be around, always a smile and a joke. Your dad and she weren't romantically involved, but they loved each other with their souls. Your dad had told her that he was going to ask your mom out. She thought your mom would be perfect for him. Lydia and your mom took tennis lessons together in middle school."

"I didn't know my mom knew her. I know it sounds too early, but I love Caleb and I know it's love. Like is too mediocre of a word to describe how I feel. How could my dad feel this way and be in a 'just friends' relationship? Is that common with Tamers?"

"All that are bound would pay the ultimate price to protect their mate, regardless of friends or lovers."

I blush at the word *lovers*, it sounds cheesy.

"This is a quick and easy way to force out good vibes to a room. Mentally close your eyes and imagine a blue light emitting from your core. Will peace and comfort to the room. It might be harder to do to a room of people. You get one person pumped up for chaos, and they fuel the room with their vibes. You're powerful enough to soothe that energy down. If you need some help, teach your friends how to do it and together it shouldn't be a problem." She takes a look at her watch and taps it lightly. "Only an hour left, I'll let you go finish up. Tonight, you need to keep your light honed in, it's rippling through you. I wonder if you're always so charged up. It is probably not wise to share with everyone how powerful you are. Even with your newfound friends, they're young and can go fickle in a blink of an eye."

She pulls me in, and kisses me on each cheek.

I open the door to the stairwell, catching Thorne scrambling to stand up. "You were eavesdropping!"

"Guarding your secrets, not spying." He points to himself. "Guardian, remember?"

"How can I forget?" As we get to the door at the bottom of the stairs, Amber looks up in time to see us leaving the stairwell.

"Hmmmm, if I didn't know better; I'd be suspicious of you coming out of a secluded room together." Amber crosses over to us carrying a tray of cheese. "Cheese madam?" She curtsied with her head bowed and the tray held out to us.

"You're the help?" Thorne teases.

"Yes sir, would you like a bite of my cheese?" She flirtatiously replies.

"I think I'm going to go check on Caleb, you kids have fun." Before I have a chance to turn around, I feel hands on my waist from behind.

His chin on my shoulder and he whispers in my ear, "You're getting too good at blocking me out, how was your lesson?"

I turn into his arms and put my ear to his chest, nothing soothes me more than the beating of his heart. *It wasn't bad. I hope we will have some alone time later. We'll get together with Amber, and I'll show you what she taught me.* I thought to him, opting to answer through our bond.

Okay, we'll go to that guest room down the hall. You and me both, I need some alone time with you too. We'll go get some ice-cream after everyone leaves and head to our favorite spot by the river. I don't mean to upset you, but what's going on with you and Thorne?

Nothing, why?

Just a vibe I get. I don't think you're cheating or anything. It seems that he watches you like a hawk. I know, because I do. Not in a freakish stalker way, in an 'I love you more than anything in the world way.'

You stalk me? That's sweet, well, yeah sweet. Aww don't worry. He's new to the area like I am, and he likes Amber, I think. We're just friends.

In my book guys that want to be 'just friends' don't stalk their friend. I'll leave it alone, but it is strange. I hope he isn't another Erebus.

No, he's an oddball, but he's fine. I turn and give him a quick kiss on the lips.

Mmmm, I can't wait to have you alone, on a blanket, watching for shooting stars and feeling your body pressed to mine.

Oh, look at my arm...you gave me goosies. I'm all twitterpated. I cross my arms and rub them to get the goose-pimples to go away. I concentrate on closing off my thoughts to him, I need my privacy sometimes. My heart skips two complete beats as I think of his last words to me.

"Oh, you play dirty," Caleb says.

I turn and put my hand over my mouth and make my eyes go wide, "Who me?" I move my hand and pout my lips. "Amber, I'll meet you in the guest room, I want to show you something." Caleb mouths the words "I love you," and I skip off to the guest room and giggle out loud.

"What's up with her?" I hear Amber say to Caleb as they trail behind me.

"She's off her rocker."

"Fo shizzle."

"Okay Snoop Dogg."

CHAPTER 15. PARTY

The family room is usually *Southern Living perfect,* now it's filled with forty or so teens. Mr Gayle borrowed folding chairs from the country club to accommodate our crowd. We'd spent the last hour setting them up and removing unneeded furniture. The weatherman issued a Flash Flood warning so we decided to have an indoor meeting.

I'm looking around the room trying to recognize everyone in their street clothes. At school, everyone looks preppy, tonight they don't. A guy in the back looks like a deranged lunatic in his top hat, shredded jeans and button down shirt with a plaid bowtie. *When did top hats become a fashion statement? Do you know him?* I think to Caleb.

Take a better look, it's Rob.

Oh my freakin' frog, it is Rob. That's hysterical. How many Mountain Dews did Amber have? She is bouncing up and down on her toes?

I think she drank a two liter, she kept going in the kitchen to get a refill her flask..

She's drinking from a flask? What the h?

She says it makes her look like she has street cred if she drinks like a gangsta.

I focus on not busting out in giggles. "I guess we should start," I say to the group. A few people are still talking, and others are staring off into space. I catch Amber's attention, and I give her the look. The one that says 'help', she winks at me and gets everyone's attention.

"HELLLLOO! Do you think we're standing up here for our health? Stop your yappin' and start your listenin'." Oh my, her country girl came out big time. She is small and doesn't look over 14, but when pushed to her limit, she's a force to be reckoned with. "Ya'll are the ones that wanted to meet on this beautiful FRIDAY NIGHT, after being around all of us all day long. So, don't be a loser, listen with your ears so we can all get on with our night. Jessie here is a New Yorker from the Bronx, she's got the mob in her back pocket. Don't think because she is quiet that she's not tough."

What is she doing? I don't know anyone in the MOB, she's delusional.

She's loving it though.

Yeah, you're right.

"Without further ado, meet Jessie."

I lean over and whisper in her ear "MOB seriously?" Her grin lights up her face with mischief. I scan the crowd and see Rob waving. "Hey everyone, I'm Jessie, and this is Caleb. We're bonded Light Tamers. Some of you were here a few weeks ago when we lost our bond for a nanosecond, and I inadvertently bonded with Clark. As you can see, it's no longer an issue." I catch Jasmine glaring at me like a tiger ready to pounce. Caleb gives my hand a little squeeze, and I calm my nerves. A girl on the second row raises her hand.

"What makes you an expert on anything? You moved here this summer, and you've been stuck at the hip with Caleb and Amber since you got here. I don't get why we have to listen to you."

I'll answer her, Caleb says. "Tammy, you're right, Jessie did move here this summer. Yes, we spend a lot of time together as well as with Amber. What makes us any different? We do have inside information, and we want Tamers to hone their skills beyond what the school wants for us. We'll all be out of school in a year or two and off to college or whatever it is life hands us. Before we have a chance to begin our journey, we have another problem." The room starts murmuring lightly. "Nyx has left the Underworld, rumor has it, she is looking for vengeance."

"For what, that little hoochie Amber?" Tammy replies. The room collectively gasps at her comment. Before Caleb answers, Thorne is up from his seat in the back row.

"Who do you think you are coming into someone's home and insulting one of their guests? You're a disgrace to Tamers, who are good and do good things. Take a minute and look at what's wrong with this world. People bully other people because they feel threatened or insecure. Amber is my friend and I highly suggest you apologize to her this instant." Thorne is standing there in front of Tammy with his arms crossed.

"Did he say disgrace? Who says that?" Caleb takes a sip from his water bottle as he watches the standoff unfold. "Tammy, I'm afraid I have to ask you to leave if you can't apologize."

"Sorry," Tammy says, not very convincing either.

"It doesn't matter why Nyx is here, what matters is getting her back to the Underworld. Our two worlds don't belong together anymore," Mr Gabe says. "Young lady, you owe Amber a better apology if you intend on staying. This is my home, and these are my son's friends and they *will* be respected. Is that understood?" His stature and delivery demand attention.

"Thanks dad. He's right, if anyone else has snide comments, please leave. We don't have time for cattiness. Nyx is extremely powerful if what the internet says is true. We're powerful too, and tonight we'll show you how to harness your light." Caleb and I are standing together, hand in hand watching everyone.

I pretend to smooth out my top when I'm actually wiping off the sweat. Caleb and I face each other, and he holds his hands out, palms down. I hold my hands under his with the palms up. "Watch what we can do." I breathe in and focus on my inner light, I sense Caleb is too. A few of the people in the back stand up to see better. My hands begin to tingle, and my heart beats so hard I'm certain I'm going to die, right now, right here.

"You're kidding! Look at the light, very cool." Someone whispers from the group.

I look over at Amber, she is standing perfectly still. "Are you ready," I say to her. She nods and holds out both of her hands, at the same time, Caleb, and I hold our hands out towards her. Caleb has one hand facing mine, I have my other hand to Amber, and she has her other hand to Caleb, a triangle of light beams. The light is soft and billowing from our hands, it feels good to have it radiating to each other. "Pull the light in." The three of us inhale, filling our lungs with air.

"That's a great party trick, but what will it *do*?" Carmen says and swishes her hair over her shoulder.

"We're showing you how you can draw light from everywhere and use it. The way it was explained to me, is when we're able to control our own emotions and light, our power will grow. Obviously we can't cure everyone or everything, but we can help as many as we can." I see several people look skeptical, but the others look intrigued.

"Why don't we start out practicing, from there, we can figure out what we can do with the light," Amber says with confidence. "I'm not trying to be a bitch or anything, but if you sit around doubting everything and not give it a try...well, you suck."

Let the good times roll.

One Hour Later

Earlier we practiced drawing in the light. Thorne had conveniently avoided practicing without drawing any attention. Amber didn't seem to mind interacting with people, which made playing with others easier. Obviously she enjoyed being in charge by the way she ordered everyone around. Thankfully, Caleb and I were the only bound Tamers. We learned that when more than four couples practiced together, the lights would surge. Mr Gabe checked the backup batteries for his emergency lighting, in case we blew the circuits. He thinks of everything.

Jess, are you feeling okay? You've been at this for over an hour. We practiced before everyone arrived, remember?

Yes, I remember. Maybe I am a little tired. It doesn't appear that I'm the only one, everyone is looking somewhat ragged. We should probably call it a night.

I concur my beautiful Light Tamer.

My pulse fluttered and my cheeks hurt from smiling so big. *I'm going in the kitchen to help them clean up. I'll leave you to clear everyone out. I heard Rob tell Amber he'd give her a ride home. I think Jersey will have a field-day with him. He's so...so flamboyant, and she's so...Jersey-Girl. Which reminds me, she has a thing for old cemeteries, and we happen to have Cedar Grove. With it being the Fall Solstice, do you mind if we go there before the dance? She's exploring her religious options, and right now she is considering Wicca. I know they honestly don't have anything to do with each other, but she wants to get a picture in front of the gate. She looked up on the web of things to do while in New Bern.*

No, I don't mind at all. It's fascinating to walk around and see the graves. The Spanish moss hanging from the trees and the gothic tombs will make a cool backdrop. She sounds cool. She's such a large part of your life, and you make a excellent friend to have. He turns me around to face him, meeting eye to eye. His pupils are lost in the darkness of his eyes. I've never known anyone with eyes so brown. *One of my mom's best friends is Wiccan, she came out and cleansed our house of negativity. Honestly, I've no idea if it worked...I know it didn't hurt.*

She must have been a great mom to have. Thank you for being so awesome, I'm lucky to have someone like you in my life.

Yeah, you are lucky…I'm a fox. He laughed and squirmed away from my sucker punch to his arm.

I round the corner into the kitchen in time to catch grandma and Caleb's dad popping each other with a dishtowel. I stand in the doorway watching them play. She might be 55, but yoga has done her figure good. Mr Gabe and Caleb go to the gym every morning at five and by the size of their guns, it is obvious. It's cute to watch them having fun together, they both deserve to be happy.

I back up and cough out loud to give them a heads up. "Do you need any help in here? Caleb is about to send everyone home." I smile to myself when I see they're standing on the opposite ends of the room. "If you have a dishtowel, I'll dry the dishes," I glance over and wink at Grandma. "Let's turn on the music and finish cleaning this mess." I scroll my lists and find exactly what a moment like this calls for…The Imagine Dragons song Its Time blares through the room. Grandma loves a catchy beat because she is obsessed with a dance move she calls *The Bump.* The only thing I know about *The Bump,* is every time she bumps my hip with hers, I get a bruise. Caleb's dad decided that he would bump my other hip making me the center to a giant bruise sandwich dance.

"What on earth is going on in here?" Amber asks as she runs over to where we're dancing. "Oh, I love this song. Look at you go Miss Gayle, show me how to do that groovy move!"

Grandma grabs Amber's hand and pulls us both into the middle of the room. We bump our hips in the front, in the back, side to side. She tells us to put our arms above our head and let the groove run through our body. We start laughing so hard my sides begin to cramp. We were caught dancing by a few of the stragglers that were looking for a way to help out. Rob runs over and bumps Amber on every off beat. The next thing you know the kitchen is full of laughter and dancing Light Tamers. Grandma semi-gracefully escapes our line of teens. She keeps saying she's going to need a hip replacement if she doesn't stop. I glance up to see Thorne brooding in the corner.

"Smile bitches!" Rob yells out and snaps a picture with his phone.

We posed, we laughed, and we lost the tension that filled the room earlier.

Has anyone told you how hot you are when you dance?

No, but I've never danced in front of anyone, with the exception of my mom. I think back to Caleb. *Where were you? I haven't seen you get your dance on.*

I'm saving it all up for the dance, I can't afford to have anyone steal my moves.

Riiiiight.

You doubt me? You'll have to beat the girls off me...

I already do!

Come on, let's close up shop. I need time alone with my hot tamale dancer.

You did not just call me a hot tamale. You're a dork.

Caleb walks over and turns off the music. "Hey everyone, we've got everything under control. Go have some fun before your curfew. I want to spend some time with my girlfriend...alone."

Grandma clears her throat.

"Alone as in sitting two feet apart and keeping our hands and lips to ourselves. Right Miss Gayle?" Caleb says innocently.

"Exactly right, except you should sit six feet apart," she teases. Everyone laughs and the sounds of car keys jingle throughout the room.

"Hey, do you and Caleb want to meet us at the bonfire? Rob and I are going. The kids from the area high schools will be there too." Amber whispers in my ear, "He has cherry vodka and said it's really good in 7-Up."

I pull away from her to search her face. "Amber, you're kidding right? You need to be careful. Don't set your drink down or let anyone else pour it and give it to you. I don't want you to be roofied. Stop looking at me like that, I'm serious. Is Rob drinking? Don't get in the car with someone that's been drinking. If you want, Caleb and I can come get you. Text me and let me know, I promise we'll get you."

"Oh. My. God. Suffer from paranoia much? I'm not going to be roofied *mom*. You're such a downer. Rob said he doesn't drink and drive, so stop worrying." She digs frantically in her purse and pulls out her lip gloss. "Stop looking at me like that. I'll be fine."

"Okay, you'll be fine. I just worry about you. Promise you'll text." *What happened to Miss Antisocial? She's becoming quite the social butterfly.*

She smacks her lips together to spread around her lip gloss. "I promise. Go make out with Caleb or something. You're so the worry wart. Bye." She leans in and fake kisses over my shoulder.

"Bye bitches. Oh girl your lips are fierce," Rob says and holds his arm out for Amber. She loops hers through his and heads to the front door.

"Don't forget!" I yell out to her. *She's going to forget.*

"Bye Jessie."

Caleb pulls me into a hug. "Don't worry, she may be *fierce,* but she's smart. She knows what happened to her brother, and she won't follow in his footsteps."

"I hope you're right."

"Eh, hem, I don't mean to interrupt, but someone's BMW is blocking my car," Thorne says.

Caleb shoots him the evil eye and says he'll go move it and walks away.

"You did a terrific job tonight. You're doing the right thing by embracing your gift and sharing your knowledge. They'll never be as strong as you, although a few of them are powerful. The more will give you a run for your money. I'm going to the beach and make sure things don't get out of hand. I don't have a radar for Amber like I do for you."

"Awe, you like her."

He grinned and pulled his key from his front pocket. "Maybe, maybe not. Go straight home. I'll pick you up at three tomorrow afternoon. Wear long pants and a tight fitting shirt with tennis shoes. You might want to bring another set of clothes too."

"Tight fitting shirt? Really?" I say disgusted.

"It's a lot easier to spar in fitted clothing. I'm not a barbarian. There's a box in your mother's closet, you'll know it when you see it, bring it. Gotta go, see you tomorrow."

"Ah, what? Box what box? Ohhhhh…how did you - never mind, I know."

I step out on the porch and wait for Caleb to finish moving the car. I'd swear I heard Thorne say *something under his breath.* Caleb bounces up onto the steps and pulls me in tight, proclaiming we're finally alone…minus one dad and one grandma.

Do you mind if we forego the ice-cream and watch a movie instead? I place my hands behind his neck and pull him in for a kiss.

Sounds good to me.

Two hours later

AMB, CALEB IS TAKING ME HOME, DO YOU NEED A RIDE?

No reply.

CHAPTER 16. SEX

5:56 a.m.

Ugh, why do I wake up before the alarm goes off? How I ended up with a morning person for a boyfriend, is beyond me. My weekends pre-Caleb were filled with blissful sleep. My father was either sleeping one off or painting in the studio (the third bedroom in our rental row house), and mom studied day and night. Since we're a bound couple, our need to be with one another every waking moment is hard for my mom to understand. Soon, I'm going to tell her what we are, she deserves the truth that her daughter is a freak of nature. I don't get how so many of us live in a house with mere humans, and no one figures it out. I never caught my dad being a Dark One and mom never realized I chazzle. I burst out laughing at the thought of her seeing me moving stuff around with my mind.

I reach over to grab my phone, no texts or missed calls.

CALL ME WHEN U GET UP! SLACKER <3

So far I'm running on time. I literally woke up, showered, stood in front of the mirror for two hundred and fifty two minutes (which translates to too long), changed work-out clothes five times and pulled my braid so tight I'll be mistaken for a tall Asian girl. Not that there's anything wrong with being Asian, but I'm pretty sure I'll have a headache by noon if I keep my hair taut.

A tapping on the door and mom peeked in, "I didn't realize you're already awake, did you have fun last night?"

"I had fun. Mr. Gabe was awesome letting us have a back to school shindig at his house. There were more kids than expected."

She smiles at me and pulls the belt on her silk robe tighter. "Would you like to go have breakfast before I head out to the hospital?"

My heart stops for a minute as guilt runs through me. Life has been complicated over this past year. Mom finished her master's in nursing and thought she'd be able to get an administrative position at the hospital. So many other nurses were vying for the same job, she couldn't find one with a salary to stay afloat. We were living off of my dad's art sales…until he moved to Greece. In New York, every other person was some type of artist, painter, musician or actor. The market was over saturated, and it was impossible to count on a steady income. Mom worked part time for a local clinic, but we needed health insurance and they didn't offer any coverage. When dad left at the beginning of summer, her heart unmistakably broke. I've been so wrapped up in my own issues; I haven't considered what pain she must be in right now.

"I'm sorry; Caleb and I are going to a workout boot-camp at the park. Why don't we have a girls day tomorrow? You...me...plus some chocolate and retail therapy. Sound good?" For a brief second, I see the look of disappointment on her face.

She plasters on a smile and pretends she isn't bothered. "Tomorrow sounds good. We'll go to Greenville and hit the mall. We'll get you shoes for the dance next month. I'm happy you've made friends so fast...I just wish you and Caleb would take it a little slower. I'll schedule you an appointment..." *She better not say birth control.* "We'll figure out what type of birth control is best for you."

She said it...why does she put me through a B.C. talk at six in the morning! "Mom, stop. I don't need birth control. We're NOT having sex. Oh Mylanta!"

"Don't Mylanta me. Jessica, I know you've promised you're going to wait, and I pray you do...BUT, and there is always a *but*...things can get out of control quickly. I know, I've been there."

I put my hand on her shoulder to give her assurance that I'm telling her the truth. "AHHHHH! LA! LA! LA! Don't talk to me about your sex life, I don't want to know." I shake my head back and forth, trying to clear out her 'been there, done that' talk. "If and when we decide to go to the next level, you'll be the first to know. I promise you. Now, if you don't mind, I need to get my stuff together to leave. Caleb will be here at seven, and he's never late." I take her shoulders and turn her around and pretend to push her to the door. "I love you, and don't forget tomorrow is mother/daughter day."

CHAPTER 17. HORSEPLAY

2:57 p.m. The same day.

AMBER, ARE YOU SO HUNGOVER YOU CAN'T REPLY!

I call my cell from the house phone to make sure the ringer is on. "Grandma, I'm not sure if my phone is working. Will you send me a text?"

YOU'RE A STRANGE KID

THANKS, I GET IT FROM MY GRANDMA!

I creep down the hall trying to sneak up on her. She's always deep in thought when she bakes. The sound of her electric mixer covers the noise I'm trying hard to avoid. Her back is to me as she is pouring an egg mixture into the bowl. After what feels like forever, I put my hands on her waist and yell, "RAAAA" in her ear.

Honestly, I almost crapped myself when she screamed. I've never seen her jump so high, or scream so loud. Fortunately she was finished mixing up the treat. Unfortunately for me, she had a giant wooden spoon in her hand. She turned around, before she registers it's me, she whacks me with the unsuspected weapon. Somehow she has grabbed my arm and is pulling it up behind my back.

"GRANDMA! You're killing me, let me go!" I half yell and half laugh.

"What's so funny? You think you can just sneak up on someone my age? I'm fragile," she says and lets go.

The doorbell chimes, I look at the clock…3:15.

"I'll get it."

"Are you expecting company?" She tosses the spoon into the sink and grabs another one out of the rooster utensil holder.

"Yeah, that guy Thorne. He's training me on self-defense. I have to protect myself from you're your beatings with wood spoons," I say trying to keep a straight face.

She wipes her hands on a dishtowel and pulls her apron over her head. "Does Caleb know about your private lesson?"

"Weeeeeell, not exactly. Please, please, please don't tell Mr Gabe. I promise, nothing is going on with us. I can't tell you, but you have to trust me." The doorbell rings again.

"Hmmmm."

He's coughing as I open the door. Removing his hand from in front of his mouth and absently wipes it on his pants. *He would be able to pass for a younger version of Ian Somerhalder. His eyes always look as if he's piercing a hole into your soul. His hair is longer than Caleb's short preppy hair...not long enough to put it up in a ponytail. Simply dressed in a fitted black t-shirt and running pants, he looks like a model.* "Sorry, I had something caught in my throat. Are you ready to go?"

"Yeah, let me get my bag." Before leaving with Caleb this morning, I grabbed the box out my mom's room. I hope I'll find some answers hidden inside. It's too bulky to carry in my backpack, so I throw it in my old tennis bag. "Bye grandma," I yell as I run out the door.

"Did you steal this car, or did it come with your imaginary house?" I buckle my seatbelt and pull the strap trying to keep it from making my boobs look strange. "You don't really live in the house do you?"

"I live there, and no, I didn't steal the car. It doesn't work if your guardian is in jail for grand theft auto. I get an allowance to take care of my needs, so I bought a car."

I wipe my hand across the dashboard. "Must be a good allowance to afford a car like this. Do you have a boss? Is there a guardian headquarters and someone sits outside waiting to see the guardian symbol in the sky, and rushes away to save the world?"

He pulls out of the driveway like a little old lady. I wave to grandma standing at the doorway watching us leave. Being alone with him doesn't bother me like I thought it would. My brain knows he's off limits for various reasons...Caleb is one of them and Amber the other.

"Your grandmother is protective, she loves you a lot," Thorne says matter-of-factly. "You're lucky to have her in your life. To answer your question, yes, I do report to someone and no, I'm not Batman."

We headed away from town, down a two lane highway I've never been on.

"Hey, how was the bonfire last night? Did Amber get wasted?"

"I don't think so. The last time I saw her, she was with that Rob guy. I went to get something out of my car, and I didn't see her again. I stayed another half hour or so, and went home. Why? Is she raging today?"

I sigh and feel something is wrong in the pit of my stomach. "I don't know. I sent her a text last night, and a few more today...she hasn't replied. Do you mind if we stop over there on our way home?"

"You should try her sister first. I'd hate for us to show up and she has used you as her alibi."

"No doubt. Good idea."

"I'm smart like that."

"Whatever."

He turns onto a driveway paved with oyster shells. I always think they will puncture the tires and cause a flat. *For someone that doesn't live around here, he sure knows his way around. Hmmm, does he have an internal GPS?*

"Where do you live when you're not saving Tamers in distress?" *Maybe he lives in heaven or another planet.*

"You're quite the talker today. My home base is in Kentucky. Where'd you think I live? Heaven?" He pulls up to single wide trailer with a cornfield front yard. "I hope you like horses."

"You didn't say anything about riding on a horse. What are we going to do, joust?"

He grabs my gym bag out of the back seat and slings it over his shoulder. He jiggles his keys until he finds the one for the front door. I'm still sitting in the passenger seat with my jaw hanging open. *I can't ride a horse. People have always said to me. Jessie, you'll put an eye out with those things. I've also heard, "If you ever go horseback riding, you better wear all the support you*

*can." I don't have said support with me. I came in yoga clothes
and a semi-tight t-shirt. He doesn't care, he's walked into the
house. Oh Lord, please don't let me fall.*

I slam my door in disgust…although it's wasted energy since I
don't have an audience. I stomp on the three wooden steps to the
front porch. I give the door as loud of a knock I can muster.

Thorne opens the door looking amused. "Are you a vampire and
need an official invitation?"

"No, I'm not a vampire, there's no such thing. I was raised not to
randomly walk into people's homes."

"You're quirky Jessie Lucentee. Come on, we need to go saddle
the horses and get to the training area. There's a pair of boots, and
some chaps if you'd like, in the guest room."

I take my bag from him and follow the direction he points.
"Chaps, you're kidding right? Who's ever heard of yoga pants and
chaps, with cowboy boots no less?"

"I gave the fashion police the day off. There are breeches if you'd
rather wear them. Size seven tall right?"

*Shoot me, shoot me, shoot me. He knows what size I wear? Caleb
doesn't even know what size I wear. Where does he get his
information?* "You suck."

"Meet me at the barn out back, and bring the box with you."

Meet me at the barn...I mock silently in my head.

When someone says *barn* and they live in a little house, I'm expecting a dilapidated shack, not a big state-of-the-art barn. The smell of horse dung and hay fill the air. Thorne is brushing a large brown and white horse. As I get closer, I can see he has already saddled the horse. The leather has a beautiful pattern of roses and filigree around the edges.

"She's a beaut isn't she?" Thorne says and holds out a baby carrot to the horse. "You're going to ride this one; she'll be gentle with you. I'm riding that one over there." He points to the other side of the barn. A beautiful black horse with a well-worn saddle looks up at us as if he understood what we were doing.

I've no idea what size horses are supposed to be, but the horse was enormous. "What's their names?"

"This one is Isis, and he is Thor."

"You named your horse after yourself?" I rolled my eyes and snickered at him.

"You don't think much of me do you? I didn't name the horse, his original owner named him." He pulled the latch on the stall and lead Isis next to me.

"What? You're not expecting me to get on a horse alone, while you're on the ground do you? I could die." Even to my own ears I sound bratty.

"C'mere, let me help you. Stop stressing about the horse; it isn't that big of a deal. I'll hold my hands out, and you're going to use your left foot to step in my hands. You'll swing your right leg up and over." Isis makes a loud protesting noise, probably aware I'm a newbie. "You'll be OK, hand me your box and I'll carry it."

I set my bag down with a silent prayer the horse doesn't squash it to pieces. I put my boot clad foot into his hands. In his miserable attempt at being funny, his hands come apart, and he yells out "MY BACK!" I didn't find the humor. After two attempts, I finally get my leg over and place my feet in the stirrups. "I still don't understand the purpose of the horses. No offense Isis," I say and pat the horses mane. "Do you mind explaining yourself?"

Thorne puts his foot in the stirrup and in one attempt he is on the horse without any problems. "Jessie, follow my lead, and nothing will happen. The walk to the training area is long and through the woods. Take the reins in your right hand. No, no, no….don't pull back like that."

I pull the reins, like they do in the movies. The horse backs up and pulls her head back in protest. Isis starts shaking her head back and forth, and I don't know what to do. I'm flustered, and Thorne laughs at me.

"You keep that up and Isis is going to throw you," Thorne says seriously.

"Huh? No, I don't want to fall and get killed. How do I hold the reins?" I begrudgingly ask in the name of not being trampled to death by a horse.

After a brief lesson on how to make the horse turn and stop, I awkwardly take the reins. The smell of pine wafted through the woods. The old pine trees are at least forty feet tall. When the winds pick up, the trees will sway back and forth. You'll hear them crack and creak and squirrels complaining out loud.

My thighs are sweaty against the leather saddle. I feel like a princess riding into battle, when in actuality I'm a kid with weird friends. The only sounds are the breaking branches beneath the horse's hooves.

"Do you hear that?" I ask.

"What?"

I look up at the trees, and see birds perched up high. They're giving new meaning to the phrase, *watch them like a hawk.* "Exactly, the silence is eerie. Do they know something I don't?"

"They probably sense that we're not human," he says matter-of-factly. "Maybe there's a predator, and their hiding."

What? Something to the right of us rustles the leaves. "Is

something over there?" I point to our right. "It isn't a bear or anything is it?"

"No, it's too early for a bear to be out for a stroll. It could be a fox or a snake. This area is known for the various species of snakes. Let's pick up the pace, I'd rather not have to go back through the woods after dark." He maneuvered Thor in front of me and Isis followed his lead.

CHAPTER 18. YOUR HIGHNESS

We enter a clearing, or an area clearer than the rest of the woods. Downed trees had been pushed to the side in a big L with a firepit in the middle. Thorne gracefully dismounts Thor and ties both horses to a small tree.

"Come on little lady, let's make you into a warrior. Put one hand on the horn and another on the lip of the saddle. Drape yourself over the side, I'll catch you."

Isis pulls her head back and bared her teeth. Horse teeth are scary looking. They're massive and strangely straight and in desperate need of cleaning. I turn and slide down her side, Thorne grabs me by the waist and lowers me the rest of the way down. His body against my back and hands on my waist give me the strangest realization. I felt nothing, absolutely nothing. No chills, no vibrations, no giddy boy touches girl reaction. I mentally sigh with relief. He's easy on the eyes, yet he doesn't hold a candle to my feelings for Caleb.

"Are you okay? Was the horse ride terrible?" He asks with a hint of concern in his voice. He spins me around to face him, his grey eyes searching mine for an answer.

I burst out laughing and playfully pushed him away. "I'm fine. Surprisingly, I enjoyed the ride. You see movies with couples riding a horse on the beach, I bet that's fun. Not saying couple as in romantic, unless I'm with Caleb and that's a different story," I ramble.

"We're not a couple?"

Awkward moment seventy-two. "No, of course not."

"I'm kidding! Stop being so freaky. I'm your guardian, nothing more. Take a few steps, I want to see you walk."

"Okaaaaay, that's weird." My first few steps are like I have Jell-O for legs, I can't seem to walk without them a foot apart. "Holy cow, what the heck? This isn't going to last forever is it? I'll have a tough time explaining this walk to Caleb, and possibly Amber." *I did not just say that! I didn't mean to imply it was sex related...he's probably thinking I'm a perv.*

Thor lifts his tail and cuts the loudest fart of any horse, anywhere in the world. I scream and run away to the other side of the clearing, laughing so hard I bend over to catch my breath. Thankfully the horse saved me from moment seventy-three.

"You're easily amused by body functions. Come on, we need to start."

"I know, I know. I'm sorry, I've never been around a thousand pound animal fart before. It was HORRIBLE! I'm ready…teach me oh mighty guardian."

He crosses his arms and holds his mouth in a straight line. He slowly walks around me in a circle, stopping every other moment to make a verbal noise.

"Why are you inspecting me like my dad picks a steak? If you begin to tell me I'm fat, I'll punch you in the throat." I smack his arm as he pretends to make a second go around. "Stop!" My voice cracks as I spoke.

Thorne raises his eyebrow. "You have such a short fuse. Do I make you nervous? Do you get the feeling you're being watched? Are your palms sweaty, and your heart racing a million beats a minute? If you're experiencing any of the aforementioned symptoms, you could be suffering from paranoia." The line of his lips starts to twitch as he holds back a smile.

"Yup, that's me…paranoid."

He uncrossed his arms, and runs his hand through his hair. "You should be. You're still thinking like a human girl without a care in the world. If this summer hasn't proven to you the extent of the danger you're in, nothing will. You still go to McDonald's, and the so-called mall, you never look around to see if you were followed. Maybe they haven't found you, and maybe they won't. It isn't like

New Bern is the tourist Mecca of the world. In a split second, your world can change. You can lose everything, including your light to the wrong person. Caleb is right to be overly protective of you. Sadly, you're easily distracted."

Sadly for yooooou. "No, I'm not." I give him my best glazed over look. "Oh, look a butterfly. I love butterflies. Bees? No, I don't like them; they scare the poop out of me. One summer I was riding my bike, and this gargantuan black dog started chasing me…I almost drove straight into five o'clock traffic. That has nothing to do with bees. I like toast."

"Funny, ha ha. I didn't peg you as a smart ass…I've changed my opinion. Back to what I was saying Miss Lucentee."

I curtsy, "Of course Mr Woodson."

"Your brain needs to take a snapshot of every moment of every day. School is a safe zone, but it doesn't mean it can't be breached. Your memory can be the one thing that will save you. I'm sure Mrs. Ward told you about Underworld dwellers not being traceable on her radar. Your ability to describe a person or share a memory with your consort will help in banishing them back to their realm."

Chills run down my spine at the thought of Nyx finding us. *Caleb my consort, what century is this?*

He walks over to Thor and removes a ratty looking blanket.

Setting it down gently next to the firepit, he unwraps the blanket, within the folds he pulls out a skeleton key.

I lean over, intrigued by the delicate scrollwork. "What does it unlock?"

"It's the key to the box you brought with you," He says seriously. "In all seriousness, my job is to protect you. Sit down; I want to tell you a story."

He crosses over and sits down on a log, closest to the elbow. I sit on the other one so I can see him as he talks. I snap a dead twig next to me and flit it around in my hand with nervous energy. "You have my full-fledged attention."

Thorne leans in; putting his forearms on his thighs and twirls the key with his fingers. "Jessie, the reason we came all the way out here to train is…this place doesn't exist. Not in your realm at least. This is a hiccup area, a portal of sorts. Did you ever read A Midsummer Night's Dream?"

My jaw clenches as the words are spoken. It hasn't occurred to me that other realms existed, except the Underworld. Stunned, I can't find the strength to talk. My thoughts are fleeting, far away from this place, to the safety of Caleb's arms. "You're kidding," I finally say.

"Nope," Thorne says and reaches for my hand.

I flinch away from him, "Don't…please." I lean forward and place my hands on my head. "My head is pounding."

"Jessie, we don't have much time. Breathe deeply and relax."

My head snaps up, and I glare at him. "You want me to relax? I'm sitting on a log, in a forest that doesn't exist as my guardian non-human protector is telling me to relax. Yeah, not going to work. I'll listen, but don't blame me for being skeptical. Explain the damn key before I jump on my imaginary horse and ride back to my imaginary town. Tell me about the quote unquote realm I'm in. Let me guess, there are faeries lurking in the trees."

"I don't think they're in the trees."

I smack my head in exasperation.

"Jessie, yes, we're in the woodlands. The most famous faerie of all time was Shakespeare. He almost dismantled the woodlands with his outing of the battles within this realm. Stop with the eye-rolling. We're safe here; well, as safe as you can be within this zone. You've been granted immunity from the Seelie Queen, unless she finds a reason to punish you. She's on good behavior for various reasons. Summer consists of Seelie fae…the good faeries. They're known to do good deeds for humans and to help right a wrong. If they're taken advantage of or mistreated, they will seek revenge. Once the fall equinox happens, the Unseelie King will be in charge until spring. Winter is stricter and is home to the Unseelie fae. The Unseelie Court is unforgiving…the King is so harsh; he has beheaded visitors for not bowing the correct way."

I sit and listen to the story about evil faeries, wanting nothing more than to leave. Thorne's face looks drawn as he tells me about the faerie courts. "They'll behead me? Let me guess…even though Summer is in charge, Winter will still enforce their rules."

"If we cross to their side, yes."

"We won't go to their side, simple. Easy peasy. None of this explains why we're out here."

"In theory it's simple. Right now, we're in a neutral area of the forest, it belongs to neither court and harbors rogue fae. The rogue and Abbey Lubbers will defend neither side without a price, and they have switched sides for the right price. We don't want to get on the Abbey's bad side…talk about ruthless. They have a vendetta against monks though and spend most of their time spying on them."

"This day gets better and better. They spy on monks, that's the strangest obsession I've ever heard."

"They're always trying to find monks not living up to their vows. Thankfully, there are only about ten of them in existence. That leaves us with the natives. Although we have the cooperation of the Seelies, it isn't acceptable to intrude into their kingdom. The

Seelie Queen has extended an invitation to meet you before the shift of power. Winter is unavailable until Summer passes the Ruler Staff to them during the harvest moon. You won't be subjected to the mischief of the Seelie fae until you've successfully closed the portal to the Underworld." His eyes go wide, and he smacks his knee. "Shit, I wasn't supposed to say that."

"What? Close a portal to the Underworld? What. The. Hell!"

He lets out a huge sigh, as he shuffles his feet in the dirt. "Yeah, don't get stuck on the technicality of little details."

"Oh, sorry, forgive me for questioning all of the freakin crazy CRAP you shovel my way. New Yorkers think they live in a world of crazy, they've no idea. Spill it, what is really going on?"

"What I tell you, must…I mean, MUST be kept between us."

I close my eyes and mentally focus on calm. "I can't make any promises. Caleb is my other half; I can't keep another secret from him."

"Oh for the love of…alright, you can tell Caleb."

"Good, we'll go get him, you can tell us together."

He shakes his head back and forth. "Not so fast, don't start jumping up and down; it will be on my terms. We'll bring him here and tell him…*tomorrow*. If Mrs. Ward finds out, she'll banish all of us to the South Pole to live in the winter court." The lines in his forehead deepen with worry. "Yes, you're expected to close the portal off. When Mr Wolfshadow had everyone do the DNA swab, it was to find a recessive fae gene. There was a band of fae who could control all of the elements, earth, wind, fire and air. In the beginning, they were plentiful, but as they mated with other fae from other clans, they weakened. It was nearly impossible for them to keep their blood pure. Light Tamers are a derivative of fire fae."

"Why are they looking for the gene? It was all a lie about finding their mate? I knew it sounded too expensive just to make people happy. What happens if they find someone with the gene?"

"We will figure out how to activate their ability and train them how to use the elements. Our survival depends on finding them. Sure, you might be able to send Nyx back to the Underworld. What will happen when the next god or goddess comes to avenge their name? This is bigger than all of us. The entire supernatural species is fighting a war, yet none are prepared for a world without Fate." He paused for a split second bumped my foot with his. "You okay?"

"I'm not sure," I answer honestly. "Go on."

"They'll help the Dark Ones grow in numbers, in turn, Tamers numbers will dwindle. Your power is strong...right now. Erebus escaping and hunting you down isn't a coincidence, he knows something...and that something may be in that box. You're only aware of a tenth of what is really out there walking the streets Jessie. Every aspect of your life will be questioned."

My heart is pounding in my ears, practically drowning out the sounds of my thoughts. "Every night before bed I stare at my nightlight and think about other magical beings. I'm always thinking about the possibilities of others like Tamers. Are the faeries here right now?"

"Yeah, they're here. Thor and Isis are magical horses that belong to the Seelie court. Without them, we wouldn't have made it into this realm. Guards set up in a circle surrounding us. They can't hear what we're saying. As a guardian, I'm granted various privileges. I required a secured site that can't be penetrated with hearing or magic." He scoots the box over with his foot, until it's in front of me. "I want you to open the box." He gently hands me the key.

"Okay," I hold my hand out to him. The key is heavy in the palm of my hand. I'd never seen a real skeleton key in person. "Is it made of iron?"

"An insurance plan to keep most fae away. Everyone knows iron is toxic to fae, but do you know why?"

"Something to do with the properties being of the earth and faeries are part of the dream world. I'm not proficient with the technical parts, they say people will eat meat because the blood has iron…it keeps the fae away." I smile confidently at his solemn face. "Don't look at me like that...I had a friend in middle school that was obsessed with the idea of faeries. I'm right aren't I?"

"Partially."

"What do you mean 'most fae'?"

"There is a breed that can touch iron."

"Interesting, what do the box and the key have to do with the portal? It isn't the portal is it?"

"No, open it, we're about to find out." He shifts his look to the trees behind me.

I twist around to see what he's looking at, "Everything cool?" He nods his head. "Why would my mom have the box? It was in her closet. My dad said she doesn't know about us, which I honestly don't get. My life is loopy! One day I'm a girl with an alcoholic father and a nursing student mother, the next, I'm in crazy-ville with front row seats."

"Open the box," he says impatiently.

"Okay, hold your panties on." My hands tremble slightly as I run my fingers along the edge. I put the key in the brass plated hole until I feel it catch. Breathing in a sharp breath, I turn the key and feel the lid unlock."

Thorne takes in an audible breath as the box opens.

Inside there are two daggers perfectly fitted into shadowed slots. Another small wooden box is wedged in the corner. I take the smaller box and slide off the lid. Two rings of gold, like wedding bands, are wrapped in silk. The rings are cold in my palm. I look up at Thorne and his eyes are huge. "Are these someone's wedding rings?"

He doesn't say anything, only nods his head.

"Holy shit! Jessie, you just found....oh, no...you couldn't have. There's no freakin' way! No wonder she has trouble with you on her radar. I never saw it coming. Well, I kinda did, but not really. This is ridiculous. I'm not sure we can wait until tomorrow to tell Caleb. I vow to you that I will protect you and serve you as long as you'll have me, your highness."

Eh? "Why are you vowing to me? Your highness? What the crap is that? What is wrong with you? Are these the Lord of the Rings rings? If I put it on, will I become evil and crouch in the corner calling it *my precious?*" I take the smaller ring and start to put it on my ring finger.

He grabs my wrist stopping me. "Don't, it isn't time for you to wear it."

I pull my arm from his grip. "You're freaking me out. Who's rings are they?"

He holds his hand out, and I set the ring in his palm. He holds the ring up, inspecting it as though he were a jeweler. I'm mesmerized by the way it glints in the sun.

"It's the proof the prophecy is true. Look, right here," he points to the inside of the ring. "Preaditi Unum."

"Don't go all Gandalf on me...what does it mean?"

"The Gifted One. That's you."

I roll my eyes and laugh. "Let me guess...I have to marry you, and we'll save the world."

He looks at me baffled. "No...you must marry Caleb."

Oh yeah...wait up! Marry him! "Will you and your magical horse take me to the looney-bin? I'm having horrible hallucinations that you told me I have to get married. It doesn't occur to you that I'm fifteen?" I pull out one of the daggers and hold it up like a serial killer. "Do we stab each other in a murder suicide with these?" Thorne just stares at me, his eyes wide and his mouth half open. I try to put the dagger back in its slot, it slips, cutting the velvet. Pulling it back, the box makes a popping sound as the bottom pops up. Under the false bottom is a small leather book. "Wow, look how old this is." I turn it over in my hand, noticing how it's worn, and oil stained from someone's hands. It's held together by a massive leather strap with a crazy looking lock. *Is this the book with our family information? My dad said he'd never seen our family book. Why would he lie to me? Maybe it isn't that book at all.*

Thorne stands up and starts pacing back and forth. He has one arm crossed and his other hand up over his mouth.

"This is the biggest thing I've ever been a part of. We're about to make history...this is caaaaRAZY. "

"You find me opening a box caaaaRAZY? Well, how about light shooting from your hands, someone having access to your every thought, a magic school with nutty teachers...oh, not to mention Fate is the principal...oh, let's not forget my dad is a light thief. You find a box crazy. You're crazy. I'm done."

"No, no, no...I didn't mean it like that, I mean it like...this is going to be epic. You're not actually the Light Tamer princess or queen...but you *are* the Faerie Queen." He annunciates every word. "The legend says that only the queen of faeries would possess the Dagger of Destiny, the Ring of Virtue, and the Book of Fae. Only the queen will be able to open the book. Try the dagger, maybe you can cut the leather."

I still my shaking hand and attempt to cut the leather. *I sure as hell don't want to use this to cut my steak.* "The knife is too dull."

He takes the knife from my hand, bends over and cuts a hunk of wood out of the log. "Nope, not dull." He hands it back to me.

"What if I stab the book? You know, like in the cartoons, when they stab a book and a light spews from it? Watch." I hold my arms above my head and bring them down as hard as I can. The dagger bounces back, and I fall over. The leather is perfectly unharmed. "I guess we're not in a cartoon. How did my mom end up with this box? Did you know what it had in it?"

"Mrs. Ward warned me the box might contain a historical object. It didn't click until I saw the rings. Why don't we call Caleb and have him meet us at your house? We can't do that until we get back to the car though... fae don't get signal or phone plans out here." He grins at me. "You can smile Jessie. This might prove to be the silver lining."

"You honestly think my mother is going to let me marry another high school student? Where does it put me on the Light Tamer scale?" I start packing the box as it was.

CHAPTER 19. GRANDMA CONFESSES

The horses whinny and like an illusion another horse appeared. The sun was setting behind the rider, making it hard to see their face. Thorne makes a motion as though he has a sword in his hand. Slowly, with his other hand, he pulls me behind him to shield me from the rider.

"Put your damn sword up. You honestly believe Nyx would ride into the woodlands and not set off some alarms? Not that she can even enter the realm. Where is Jessie?"

I push Thorne to the side. "Grandma?"

"What have I said about that word?"

"Miss Gayle, how did you find us? How did you get in?" Things just went from weird, to weird with a twist of insanity. I look back and forth between the two.

"Young man, what's your assignment ID?" Grandma asks. She stands there in her designer jeans and cowboy boots. *I've never seen her wear cowboy boots before.* "Are you mute?"

"2 2 5 7 2 T as in tango, G as in green," Thorne puts his hands on his hips.

"Grandma, how did you know where we are?"

"Oh, Jessica, it's complicated."

I pop my fingers. "I'm beginning to wonder what isn't complicated. Please tell me I'm dreaming."

"I heard you were here from some old friends. I intended to be with you when you opened the box. Your pet bozo over here decided to sneak you in here, tell you… get Caleb and pretend he discovered you."

I turn and look at Thorne. "Is that true?"

"He can't lie to you…can you Thornathan?" She raises her eyebrow at him. "I've heard rumors about you. I hear you walk the line with rules."

He cocks his head, "*I walk the line? Are you the pot calling the kettle black?* You think I don't know about you? Your *friends* told me all about you. You've been hiding away all these years, not even visiting your father. Did you tell her you were adopted, and why?"

I see how uncomfortable she's getting. "Stop! Both of you. I don't know what's going on, and I'll get the full story. I'm assuming you're a Light Tamer." My hand won't quit trembling as

I run my fingers through my hair. "You told me about your brother and the way you had a bright yard. Why? All this time you knew." *Don't cry...no.* The tears sting my eyes and I will them away. She comes over to me with her arms out wide. I instinctively pull away. "No, stop."

Thorne steps away as she puts her hands on my shoulders. "I'm not a Tamer hun. I'm half fae. My mother was human, and my father is fae. He used glamour to look human. At the time, he was only a prince, and it was taboo to have relations with humans...even though it happens more than you think. He was the firstborn son to the king, and he was next in line to get the crown. My mother died when I was two months old. My father couldn't have me live with him in the Woodlands, so he found a family to adopt me. My adoptive mother had known my real mother, and she knew about my dad. The agreement was, my dad could visit me a few times a month. He would sneak me into the Woodlands and let me play with the fae in the forest. He swore everyone to secrecy, and they made a blood pact. His brother had suspicions about my dad; he wanted the crown left to him. He found out about me and told their parents. They banished my dad to the forest to live among the Woodland fae. No, I don't see my father any longer. If guardian boy over here knew anything about living on this side of the shiny shimmer, he'd know why." Her shoulders slump and sadness fills her face.

I throw my arms around her and say softly, "It's okay, I love you.

How am I a queen then? If it's a bloodline kingdom, how do I fit in?"

"Yes, in those type of kingdoms…*you're* destined. A fulfilled prophecy trumps bloodline. I've protected you as long as I can. Now you know the truth, I will make sure you and Caleb are crowned."

"You want me to marry him too?"

"It isn't up to me."

"How on earth am I going to get my mom and Mr Gabe to agree to us getting married?"

Turning to face her, I see how the lines in her face are gone. Her hair is longer and rich with color. Taking her hand in mine, the veins aren't popping out. She looks twenty-five years younger and by the way she moves, she feels it to.

"We'll get Caleb and bring him here; it will be easier to tell the story once."

I mentally scan for him, trying to pick up any type of connection, to no avail. The void is almost insufferable. When we block each other from our thoughts, we still have the connection. It's as though we have an invisible lifeline to one another. Right now, my lifeline is missing.

Thorne is kicking around a rock. "Stop pouting. I need to see

Caleb…and find out why Amber hasn't returned my calls." I kick a rock at his boot.

"He's in the car."

"Caleb's in your car? Why didn't you bring him with you?" I ask.

She took in a deep breath. "I wasn't sure what I was about to walk in on."

I gasp, "Grandma!"

"Not like that! I wasn't sure if anyone figured out who you are and kidnapped you," she insisted. "He's already freaking out because he doesn't feel your bond with him."

"Oh no, I didn't think about him not having contact. I've been here forever; it has to be after dinner. When did you leave?"

"He and I came after you about thirty minutes after you left. I realized the box was gone when Caleb called to see if you were home. I had a feeling the tomfool *guardian* brought you to the shimmer." She turned to glare at Thorne.

"Look, we ALL have the best interest of Jessie as our priority. I can't operate properly with your hostility towards me," he says through gritted teeth.

"Hostility? You have no idea how hostile I can be," she growls back.

I throw my hands in the air and storm off towards the horses. I tune out their bickering and focus on how I'm going to mount Isis. The horses stepped sideways, and Isis stepped back until she is lowered down enough for me to mount her. I've never seen a horse bow before, I've never seen a horse do much of anything. I climbed onto the saddle, and she stood up straight. Isis walked until we were a few feet from the clearing. For some reason, I can't hear them. His arms are flailing, her hands are on her hips, and their mouths are moving but no sound. Without warning, the two turns and look at me, both surprised.

"Why can't I hear you?"

Grandma mouths, "What?"

Thorne's face cracks into a smile. With a wave of his hand, the sound is back. He shrugs his shoulders.

I glare at them, not sure what's going on.

"We need to leave," he says. "It'll be dark in the Woodlands within the hour. Come on, we can't leave the same way we came."

"You're a strange guy. I liked you better when you were the mysterious guy with the hoodie and untied Docs. Why can't we go back the way we entered?"

"In case you're being followed…the fae are superstitious about things like that."

I roll my eyes. "I'm ready - get the bag and we'll leave." From the corner of my eye, I see grandma mounting her horse…faerie..horse-faerie? Whatever …is it always a horse?

CHAPTER 20. TRUTH

When a house finally comes into view, I realize it's a house we passed right before we turned off the road. I thought he was going to make us appear somewhere far away.

Grandma's convertible is parked next to Thorne's car. The instant I spot him, his head turns to me, and it breaks out in a smile. My heart skips seven beats and relief washes through me. *Hey Mr Baldwin, I'm so glad to see you!*

Hello beautiful, are you okay? Did he hurt you?

No, we need to talk. Thorne and grandma have news for us. Get ready for crazy.

Crazy huh?

Yup. We're putting the horses up, come out back to the barn.

Caleb grabs my waist and helps me down from the horse. His hands never leave me; instead, he pulls me in for a hug. Stroking my hair, he whispers about how worried he was. I shuddered from the chills he sends through me.

"You should wear cowboy boots more often. You're pretty hot as a cowgirl."

"Awe, I bet you say that to all the girls."

"You're kidding...you truly are sappy as hell. Amber said you two were sappier away from school, and she's right," Thorne complains.

"Amber! I need to call her." I check my phone for signal, and it says 4:00. "Can I use your phone - mine is confused." Caleb hands me his phone, I'm stunned when I see it says 4:02. "Something must be wrong with phone signals or something. Your phone says its only 4:02, I know we were gone for a few hours."

"Oh yeah, time doesn't pass on the other side of the shimmer," Thorne blurts out. "Give me a second and we'll go talk."

Caleb looks at me curiously, "Shimmer?"

"Let me call Amber, and I'll tell you what the shimmer is." Amber's phone goes straight to voicemail. "Damn, voicemail. Where do you think she went?" Caleb and Thorne just look at me and shrug. "Glad to know you're so concerned."

"I'm sure she's fine, probably drank and got grounded. Her dad would have called you if she were missing. Don't stress...I'm sure she has a big story for us on Monday morning." Caleb says as he pulls me into a hug and kisses the top of my head. "Miss Gayle, do you think Amber's okay?" Thorne asks grandma as though they're best buds.

"I'm sure you're right."

Thorne isn't good at hiding his concern, it's written all over his face. He motions for us to follow him. It feels like it's been hours since I was inside these walls.

"I'm going to brew some coffee, would you like any?" Thorne asks us as he fills the carafe with water. After a unanimous yes, he and grandma set mugs and coffee creamer out on the dining table. He pulls a bag of Milano Cookies with dark chocolate out of the cabinet. Grandma takes the cookies and puts them on a plate, setting it in the middle of the table.

The dining table is much smaller than the one at home. I doubt anyone has used it before; the finish is perfect, not as much as a nick to be seen.

"I'm feeling like something major has happened, I can't put my finger on it though. Would someone like to enlighten me?" Caleb's voice is cool without a hint of frustration, although I could sense that he was.

"Okay, here's the deal dude...I'm not a Light Tamer. I'm a guardian, and I've been assigned to watch out for Jessie. In the beginning, I thought it was odd to watch a Tamer. I mean, well, there isn't too much drama that goes along with them. Typically, the Dark Ones do their thing and go. They don't haunt a family and don't usually do serial light stealing. If the teachers had their way, they'd make you guys think it happens all day, every day. So yes, I was confused about the Jessie assignment. I find out after I get here about her heritage, and that made more sense. It wasn't until this afternoon that everything came together, crystal clear."

"You're an angel?"

Thorne sets his mug down harder than necessary. "No, I'm not a damn angel. Why does everyone think that you take the word guardian and associate it with an angel? I'm far from angelic...I do, however, have a code of ethics, just as they do. Trust me when I say, it isn't much fun guarding someone who is bound to a big dude that looks like he can kick my ass. Not that I can't fight, but I'm not into fighting for a girl. Don't get me wrong, I'll fight for her, but not for her in the relationship kind of way. She's not my type." He looks over at me and my mouth drops open. "You're too pretty, too sweet...too...good. I like my love interest to be edgy and spunky."

"Like Amber?" I grin from ear to ear as I say it.

"Like Amber," he agrees. Grandma and Thorne begin by telling Caleb about the woodlands and grandma's secret.

The next hour was spent telling him about the box and its contents. I open it again and show him the smaller box with the rings. Everything was going smoothly, up until they tell Caleb we have to get married….because we're going to rule Fairyland.

"We can't get married; she's not sixteen yet. I don't think you can get married in North Carolina at fifteen," Caleb complains.

You don't want to marry me?

No…yes…yes I do, but not like this…not right now. We can't vote or get credit, we can't support ourselves…this is a dumb idea.

I scoot my chair closer to him, he puts his hand under the table, and I take his hand in mine. *You're right. You were so adamant; I thought maybe you didn't see us together in the future.*

Jess, don't be silly. We will be together for the rest of our lives. I love you, you're a part of me…I'm nothing without you. It might sound corny, but it's true.

"Are you paying attention? I'm not here to talk to myself. When is your birthday Jessie?"

"August thirty-first." The three of us say in unison.

"That's Friday, we can't wait for Friday. Honestly, your age isn't a big deal in the super world," Thorne says matter-of-factly.

Caleb and I turn to each other and back at Thorne. "Super world?"

"You know… the supernatural world."

"Oh yeah, that world…I totally forgot. What does this world consist of?" I ask sarcastically.

"Sorry, that's a need-to-know basis…right now you don't need to."

I huff and turn to grandma. "What kinds of supernaturals? He might not be able to lie, but his omission isn't the truth." She shakes her head at me. "Explain this Fairyland prophecy. How does Light Tamer fall into the category of faerie?"

"That's the easy part. All magical beings get their powers from the elements. Your light is a gift and to those who went dark…their curse. Like the Seelie and Unseelie Courts, one predominately good, the other not-so-good. There's been many presages about leaders of courts, packs, clans, congregations to come. Each has slowly been brought to fruition over the last decade. The fae have exclaimed the presage about them was just a fairytale…pun intended. They guessed since they don't operate on a parallel realm, they wouldn't need to worry about the so-called prophecy. Growing up with a human family and visiting the Woodlands, I was intrigued with the stories the rogues would tell. You may have noticed when we were on the other side of the shimmer, I was younger. Fae don't age like humans. We start as children and age to no more than thirty - physically. You'll meet fae who are hundreds and hundreds of years old. I'm relatively young compared to them. I'm not jaded by the rules and regulations of their world. I've never lived on the other side of the shimmer. I actually found their stories intriguing, and the elders love to tell their stories. One of them gave this box to me when I was about your age Jess. He wanted me to try to open it, obviously I couldn't. He told me to keep the box, one day I'd have reason to try again. I had the box in the closet before you and Tabitha moved in. When I got wind there was a Guardian involved, a nice omission Mrs. Ward left out, I knew the time had come. Lucky for us, he came with a key," she said pointing to Thorne.

"Where did you get the key?" Caleb asks Thorne.

Thorne stood to cross the room; he picked up a messenger bag. The khaki bag was well-worn with frayed edges and stains. He pulls out a journal looking book. "This is a book assigned to guardians. The book fills with information regarding my next charge. Each evening, I talk to the book, and it documents my words. The information is stored for reference if needed. Once the assignment is over, the book goes blank…until you receive the next name. Sometimes, I'm called to work another case. The new guardian will receive all of my notes when their book reveals the name. That's what happened to me. I was on a mission when Jessie's name appeared in the book. When one assignment trumps another, it's usually important. The notes stated I was told to talk to a fae by the name of Locke. He's…"

"Nuts," Grandma blurted out.

"Yeah, we'll go with that word. He gave me the key, and said the Lady of the Lake told him to retrieve the key. He had to go to the bottom of her lake and was rewarded with a kiss. He was chattering on about her beautiful smile, the way she hovered over the lake, in a gossamer dress."

Grandma pours herself a fresh cup of coffee and shakes her head. "Granted a kiss did she? Obviously he hasn't collected on the kiss, or he wouldn't have given you the key."

"Why, what does a kiss do?" I ask.

"One kiss will link him to the lake; he'll lose his earth magic, and become a water wielder. Water is cool, but when you've lived three hundred years roaming the forest…losing your magic will kill a fae like him."

"Oh, how terrible. She has him get a key made of iron and rewards him with death? Who does that?" I blurt out.

Thorne squished his face as if he smelled something foul. "The fae are losing nothing when it comes to him, trust me."

Grandma shakes her head in agreement about Locke. "How did you find out the box was at my house? I didn't even know."

"The book, it said to tell her to bring it."

"What is in Kentucky if you get all of your info via book?"

"Home," he says, without any hint of betrayal to his secrets.

"When I don't have an assignment, I live in Lexington. I haven't been back to Kentucky for anything other than meetings. My roommate is a slacker when it comes to being a guardian; he's on suspension for failing to protect his charge. She died before she was slated to, which tethered her soul to earth. Until he finds a necromancer to successfully release her to the heavens, he is suspended. It is no bed of roses to have a soul stuck in limbo, and stuck with you. Since he's at fault, she stays with him...constantly! I hear she's a chatterbox. She talks non-stop while he's trying to sleep, going to the bathroom, entertaining a lady friend. You get the idea."

"Miss Gayle, what is the prophecy?"

My phone buzzed with a text.

WHAT IS WRONG??

I was worried.

I'M FINE.

Good, put this address in your GPS and come here...NOW

DO YOU HAVE ASPIRIN?

You hung over?

STOP BEING THE ALCOHOL POLICE

When can you get here? Thorne is here.

OH?

When will you be here?

IF YOU HAVE ASPIRIN I'LL BE THERE IN TEN MINUTES

"Does anyone have aspirin? Amber said she'd be here in ten minutes if we have some."

"I have some in my car," Grandma replied.

WE HAVE ASPIRIN. COME ALONE.

K

"I'll give you the short version of the prophecy."

"Wait - you don't Amber here to hear the story?" I ask, my eyes meeting his.

"Jess, I think it's better you hear this without the peanut gallery and her comments."

"Grandma, you did not just call her the peanut gallery."

"You did not just call me grandma! I call a spade a spade."

Caleb shakes his head in agreement.

"Okay, spit it out."

"As you'd have it Your Highness. The box you opened has two daggers, the Dagger of Destiny has been spoken about through the centuries. The leather on the handle of the daggers is made from hide that was tanned with a thousand tears shed by angels when Christ was born. It is told, the crowned nobility who uses the daggers will be the victor of any battle fought for the greater good. They won't bare their powers until the Ring of Virtue is placed upon the true King and Queen of Faeries. Anyone to dare try on the ring without being virtuous and pure of heart will fade away as sand to the ocean waves. They will not return to the earth to fulfill their decedent's magic. The final ingredient is in the book. The Book of Fae has been rumored to exist for as long as history goes back. I'm certain, this is the book. I was thinking about the reason you weren't able to open the book…you aren't the Queen…yet. The prophecy says the guard will go behind his masters back and help crown the Queen. Of course, everyone believes the Queen is already of royalty…you know, having guards and all. I'm the guard. I'm the guard. Oh holy hell, I'm the guard. I'm in the prophecy too." He runs his hands through his hair over and over. "Oh this is bad, very, very bad."

"Why?" We ask.

"The betrayal will be paid with a sword to the neck!" He runs his finger across his throat.

"Oh my. You get beheaded? That's horrible." I state the obvious.

"That's not all…you're the one who does it."

"Me?" I point to myself. "I'm not cutting anyone's head off Thorne. I assure you that isn't happening."

"It is as it shall be Your Highness; I am here to serve you for as long as I have a head."

"You're a riot. We don't know that we're the King and Queen."

"You are, and I will be officiating the nuptials. Now I know why I had to take that online class. Someone knew this would happen, it doesn't make any sense, but I know this is true. You're the destined royalty, and I am here to protect you...up until you kill me."

"Stop saying that. I'm not killing you!"

"Well, he might." He points to Caleb.

"I'm not killing you. What else does the prophecy say?" Caleb asks.

"The King and Queen of Fairyland will stand alongside other leaders of many bloodlines. The stance is for the safety of humans and all humanity," he says excitedly. "You must believe me when I say, you have no idea what type of powers are spread across the world. Every tale you've ever read and some...and plenty have truth to them. Those beings do exist, and some are very bad and incredibly ruthless. The sooner we perform your vows, the sooner we can announce your existence throughout Fairyland."

"Will Caleb and I be safe in Fairyland? You talk about these other so-called supers and how ruthless they are, well, can they harm us?"

"Yes love, you'll be safe, for the most part." She holds up her hands to keep me from asking another question. "Once your Court is announced and brought forth, you'll be safe. Anyone from your Court who betrays their vow to you, will be beheaded. Treason isn't taken lightly. The fae from the other Courts...that's another story. The Unseelie Court will continue their rule over winter and the Seelie Court over summer. We're approaching the fall equinox, which means the Unseelie will be coming and going through the shimmer. Once they are in this realm they lose much of their power, not all of it though. Much of the severe changes in weather are caused by sylphs. They're little faeries who control air, wind and rain. The winter sylphs of the Unseelie Court like to cause drama for the world. Interesting enough, they work all year long. There are four hemispheres on earth, there are two in Fairyland, Northern and Southern. The dominant hemisphere is the Northern one. I veered off subject. The fae that are in our realm aren't as strong, don't let it fool you, they're tricky. If a shape shifter were to capture a fae and bind them with iron chains, the fae will either die a gruesome death, or they agree to the demand. Once they shake on the deal, it is owed. Never say anything like, I owe you one...or I promise. The troubles those sayings can cause a kingdom.

Grandma reaches across the table for my hand, I gladly give it to her. "Honey, we'll figure this out…until we do though, you have to marry him."

My nerves are shot, my head is spinning and tears are two seconds from tipping out of my eyes. "I'm not ready to be a wife, in wifely ways. Mom isn't going to buy into this wedding. My dad will flip out, really flip out."

By the look on her face, grandma knows what I mean about not ready. "Jess, you don't consummate the marriage. The rings of virtue will only work as long as you are…well…a…virgin."

She said *it*, she said the *word*. Out loud she said virgin. I look at Thorne, and he has his best straight face on, as well as ears which are beet red. "Yes, I'm a virgin. Big news, we can rent a skywriter to say JESSIE IS A VIRGIN."

The door is practically ripped from the hinges as Amber bursts into the trailer. "Now this is my kind of party. Who's the virgin?" Amber blurts out before realizing Grandma is sitting across from me. Her hand goes up over her mouth in embarrassment.

"Sit, silent and listen," Thorne demands.

Amber grins and sits on the other side of Caleb.

"We'll get you caught up with everything, but first we're all hearing about the faerie prophecy," I say. "Want some coffee?

This is a fresh pot."

"Aspirin and coffee." She props her head up with her hand.

Oh, hungover Amber is a tamer, gentler, creature. *She looks like hell.*

Yeah she does, Caleb thinks back to me.

"Will you be my maid-of-honor?"

"Eh?"

"Will. You. Be. My. Maid. Of. Honor?"

Her head flips back and forth, looking for an answer on someone's face.

"Okay, I guess I'm buying a ticket to ride the crazy train. Sure, I'll be whatever you want me to be. Can I be the flower-girl too?"

"When is the wedding?" I turn and look to Thorne for an answer.

He takes his phone out and punches in something… "Hmmm, looks like tomorrow will be good. I'll secure the clearing, and we'll take care of the wedding. Between now and then, I want you all to stay together. Amber will it be okay for you to stay over with Jessie? I'll meet you here, and we'll ride to the shimmer together."

"What is the *shimmer*?" Caleb asks.

"It's the entrance to an alter realm, the one where faeries live. Thorne is a guardian and has been assigned to Jessie. His job is to protect her against any threats. Nyx doesn't have access to the woodlands, which are located in Fairyland. After you're married, your castle and the court will appear. The prophecy specifically speaks of the shift in the realm. There will be turmoil, especially over you two growing up human. The Light Tamers are regarded as healers, and most are respected. Your Tamer quality is the fae in you. I too am half fae. I've never lived on the other side of the shimmer, but I've visited many times. Fairyland respects the Tamers and the good they do for humans. Their beef is the fact fae have reproduced with humans. It all makes perfect sense now. Nyx isn't concerned about Erebus, she is worried you'll take your thrown and banish the Underworld from ever returning to the earth. Once the ring is on your finger, the dagger will guide and protect you on your journey.

"Dagger of Destiny, the Ring of Virtue, and the Book of Fae. Only the queen will be able to open the book. Try the dagger, maybe you can cut the leather."

"I've tried and failed. I'm guessing here, but what if we can't open it until we're....you know...married?"

"That's a good chance. I know we have to be virtuous to wear the ring...does that mean we'll never...eh...well..." Caleb says shyly.

"Have sex? Spit it out," Amber laughs.

Oh my goodness, you didn't go there.

I did. One day, we'll want to do that..we won't be kids forever.

I know. I turned off his ability to hear my thoughts. My heart was hammering against my chest.

Grandma sits stiff as a board. "Yes, you will be able to be adults…eventually. The prophecy says you must be a virgin when you put the ring on. It talks about how young are and later says; one day your offspring will enforce your rulings. Everything will be fine. We need to go though. I'm more equipped to protect you at the house."

"You are?" I blurt out.

She bends her head forward, peering over her reading glasses. "Oh yeah, I'm prepared."

"Alrighty, I guess we'll head to Jessie's. It will give her a chance to write her vows. You have to do that don't you?" Amber prods me.

"No, she'll repeat after me. The ceremony is specific, so we won't be veering off to the left," Thorne stops and remembers something. "Jessie, you'll need to wear something blue, and it can't be seen by anyone other than Caleb. You don't have to worry about the human superstition about not seeing your beloved before the I do's." He looks Caleb in the eye. "You do love her?" Caleb shook his head up and down. "You'd die for her right?" Caleb agreed. "You might be tested, you trust her don't you?"

"What are you getting at?"

"He's telling you there might be times that you have to trust your spouse. In Fairyland, the Queen is the ruler...unless she's dead. Typically in a royal wedding there will be tests, and you'll have to trust yourself to believe in your wife. Everything is mystical, even your castle is hidden from all fae...until you're crowned."

"We have a castle? What is it called?" I ask. "You're the one that knows the prophecy; I'm assuming you know where our hidden house is. Not house...*castle.*"

"Your kingdom is currently The Hidden City of Everlasting Light. When you're crowned, it will be The Kingdom of Everlasting Light. No one knows where it is. The fae who live there have never been seen, and the powers have been guarded so well, the elders have only speculations. I'm not kidding, when I say everything is about to change." Grandma pulled me in for a hug.

As we walked out of the single-wide mobile home, something in the air swirled around us, and I felt trouble brewing. We walked in silence to the cars, I rode with Thorne...he's my guardian after-all. Caleb and Amber rode in her Jeep. Her muddy Jeep. Hmmm

CHAPTER 21. MUDDY

"Tell me something, do you wonder what Amber was out doing? Her Jeep is mega-muddy, especially for someone who makes out with the car daily. Don't ask." Thorne and I'd been driving for about five minutes before I worked up the nerve to ask him.

He taps the steering-wheel and shrugs his shoulders. "Jessie, I can't worry about her right now. You should be focusing on staying out of trouble for the next five hours. I mean it, don't go out for anything. I have two fifty pound bags of salt in the trunk. When we get to the house, I want everyone to take salt and do the protection spell. Does Caleb have any aversion to climbing on the roof?"

"Why? You're not making him sleep out there are you?"

"What? Why would I make Caleb sleep outside Jessie? Remember, you're going to the chapel to get married?"

"Chapel? They have church in Fae-ville?"

"Fae-ville?"

"You know, like Who-ville. Let me guess, you aren't into Dr. Seuss. Why do you want him on the roof?"

"I need him to send up some solar flares to notify my spaceship to land."

I choke on the mouthful of water from my now, very hot bottle of water. "Your what?" It comes out more hysterical than I expected. "You're messing with me!" He nods his head at me. "Jerk," I smacked his arm.

"Ow! You're violent for being the so-called Queen of Fairyland. You're going to be a tyrant aren't you? You'll behead random pixies that flit into your territory."

"No, I'd never do anything to hurt someone. Is there a possibility that you'll ask Amber out? Can you date her?"

"Look Jessie, I do want to take her out...right now, isn't a good time to get involved. My main concern is to guard you and Caleb. Don't go running your mouth or anything, but if the prophecy is true, I'm hanging around for a while. Unless you behead me...if you do, it won't work out for us."

"You're impossible."

"I've heard that before."

We chatted for a few more minutes about what he needs done on the roof. He wants the chimney checked and salted, as well as any other openings. We finally pull onto a street I recognize. Both of us found peace, lost in our own thoughts until we get home.

"Jess, one more thing, please don't push the Amber thing...when it's a good time, we'll see. Okay?"

Rolling my eyes, I agree. "Hey, why five hours?"

"That's when you're getting married."

"Oh yeah, silly me." I storm off to the house to grab some cups for the salt. I hope she has a way to explain why we're salting the house like a giant french fry. Hold up, did he say five hours?

Thorne left to take care of guardian guarding stuff, stuff. He'd been quiet while we salted the yard. Amber and I decided to watch The Princess Bride. I popped some popcorn and made us all a glass of sweet-tea. I'd found a taste for the sugary tea after I left the hospital. Grandma and Caleb went out on the back porch to have a private talk about the way of fae. Mr Gabe called to say he is on the way over to stay the night. I can't imagine what crazy story we'll tell my mom. *Hey mom, did you have a long day at work? Well, I can't make it to breakfast with you, sorry...but you see, I'm a faerie. Yes, you heard right, I'm fae. Oh, I forgot to mention light shoots from my hands, my bad.* I ran the scenario in my head and realized she is going to put me in therapy. *I can hear mom telling the doctor I'm having hallucinations.* I smack my forehead in denial.

"Scoot over Amb, snack lady coming through," I say and set the serving tray down on the coffee table. "What happened with you last night? Thorne said you disappeared. I sent you text messages, and you never replied."

"If you're going to grill me about last night, I'll go home. You're not my mom."

I look at her, trying to figure out why she's so hostile. "Amber, I'm not trying to be your mom. I was worried…forgive me for giving a crap about your welfare. I happen to like you, even though you can be a…" I stop myself before saying something mean.

"You were going to call me a female dog. You were, I see it all over your face."

"Maybe I was, you know damn good and well that's what you're acting like."

Amber rolls her eyes and cocks her head back. "You do like me don't you?"

"Of course I do, why would you ask?"

She reaches in her hobo style purse and gets her wallet. Thumbing past some receipts she pulls out two folded up pieces of notebook paper.

"You swear you won't make fun of me?"

"No, I wouldn't make fun of you. Amber, what's wrong?"

"This is going to get heavy; can we go in your room, in case they come back inside the house?"

We pick up our drinks and head to my room. I love that it still smells like the cucumber-melon candle I burned earlier. We both hop up on my queen size bed. Usually, we lay on our backs and stare at the shooting star ceiling.

"Okay, here's what happened. Yes, I went to the bonfire. I had fully intended on drinking Rob's vodka and getting wasted. I've thought about nothing else for the last 365 days of my life...taking a bottle of vodka and getting trashed. Like he did...my brother Mark. He was seventeen and would have been his senior year. We were all going to the beach for one last family weekend with us all as kids. He had been known as a partier...he was good looking, and one of the best surfers on this coast. This guy Randy, he had been the one with a fake I.D. and bought all the alcohol for the parties. Randy is a prick, no other word for him. I never liked him, and Mark would say I should give him a chance. I didn't think he was a very loyal friend. He was so arrogant...I mean he was an ass." She smirks as she talks about him. "Randy showed up at the beach that day. He kept asking Mark if he had the vodka with him. They were talking about it was going to be my initiation into party life, to get me drunk. I told Randy to go to hell. I told

Mark he couldn't drink, we were with our parents. I mean, crap Jess, he wouldn't have ever thought of getting drunk around our parents. I didn't see him drink, I thought he put it up…he didn't." Amber sat on the edge of the bed and bent over with her face covered by her hands. She sat there for a second trying to compose herself. "He was a freakin awesome surfer. Every surfer up and down the Atlantic coast knew my brother was the craziest and best. When you're at the beach, it's common to keep an eye out for other people in the water. He saw dad go under and not resurface. Rip currents are serious this time of year. Mark went running out to get him, but he didn't take a board with him. He'd got to dad and pulled him to shore, but he went back out to get dad's board and drowned. He died because of me." Her head dropped, and she couldn't hold back the tears.

I put my arm over her shoulder and my heart breaks in a million and seven pieces for her. "Amber, it isn't your fault. They were dumb boys…it isn't your fault."

"I know…I can't help it though. I've tried to tell myself it isn't, but it never works. Last night, I got a ride home to get the Jeep. I went down to the beach. I'd written him a letter, and planned to throw it out to sea. I didn't. We hated finding trash in the ocean. I could hear him in my head telling me how dumb it is to litter. I started crying on the way home and drove into a big muddy ditch. I told my parents we went to help someone pull their car out a ditch. I didn't want them to know how much I've been hurting.

Jessie, I should have gone after my dad. The doctors don't know what's wrong with him, technically, there isn't anything wrong. Mom thinks he blames himself and has given up." She unfolds the paper. "I'll read it to you, I'm sorry if it's dumb."

"Never be sorry for your feelings. I'd love to hear it."

"Dear Mark,

Hey bro, long time no hear. Well, you're probably wondering why I'm writing this letter. The therapist said that I'd feel better if I wrote you a letter. Look, I don't know why you drank that day. I wonder if drinking can actually hide the pain, but everything I read about it says it will only cause more problems. All year, I heard people talking about how the parties are no fun without Mark Edwards. Everyone quit talking to me because they didn't know what to say to someone like me. I've never been Miss Popularity, but it's never been like it was the last school year.

Things have changed bro. Last year, I met a new guy at school named Caleb. At first I thought he was hot, until I realized he doesn't surf. He was polite, and we hung out a few times - but we're just friends. This summer, Caleb met this girl, her name is Jessie. He brought her over to the house after he told her she's a Light Tamer (like you and me). He'd told me they were bound when they were kids, it happened on a beach one summer when she almost drowned. It made me think of you. Her name's Jessie, and she's very pretty. She has these green eyes that light up when she smiles. I feel a connection with her, I've never had with a girl. No, not in a lesbo way. She's a near drowning survivor, and I'm a drowning survivor, we click like friends should. I have a friend Mark, a real friend. We're finding out some crazy crap about this whole Light Tamer sickness. I wish I could introduce you, I think you'd be friends too.

I miss you Mark, more than words will ever express. I never thought I'd laugh again, but I do and I can. We never heard from Randy again, I told you he isn't a friend. Well, I gotta go. Could you watch over me and maybe give me a sign, a little sign that you're okay? We all miss you so much. I hope you're hanging ten, and every day is a great day for the beach. I love you."

She looks up at me, and we're both crying. I've never felt someone's pain through their words until now.

Jessie are you okay? I hear Caleb in my head.

Yeah, we'll be out in a minute. I love you.

Okay...you're not crying because we're getting married are you?

No, she told me about her brother.

Oh, okay.

"Jessie, will you live in the fairy world all the time? I feel like I just found you, and now you're going to bail on me."

I stood. "C'mere, you need a hug."

We hug, I pull away but still have my hands on her shoulders. She is so short, she literally has to look up at me. I silently pray for her soul to heal, as I do, my hands begin to glow. I see light flow all around her. The knock on the door pulls me out of the moment.

"Come in," I say.

"What happened? The pain in my heart has dulled," Amber looks up at me with her big doe eyes. "Thank you for not taking the pain all the way away. It reminds me how vital it is to follow your dreams and not make lousy choices."

"That was intense, I don't know what happened, it just....well, it just happened."

With him in the room, his energy pulls me to him. When we're alone, we gravitate to each other. His face full of concern for Amber looks to me for guidance. Like a magnet to metal, he crosses the room and throws his arms around both of us.

"Stop, ya'll are suffocating the Amber," she says as she tries to pull away from his grip. "This is so unfair, I'm at chest level here...you're not going to like it if I decide to bite your boob!"

I jump back before she makes good on her promise. "You wouldn't dare."

"I would, and I'd hold my phone out and take a pic for you."

Caleb is laughing, and the room fills with love. Relief washes over me for Amber. Never in a gazillion years, would I want to lose her to the darkness.

CHAPTER 22. SOMETHING OLD

"Wake-up beautiful, we're leaving soon," Caleb's voice whispers in my ear.

I roll over to my back, pulling the covers partially off Amber. She pulls on the blanket until she has enough to cover her face. He is standing over me, his face only a foot away. Fear runs through me as I realize I have morning breath. I try holding it so he can't smell my icky stench. I fake yawn so I can cover my mouth with my hand.

"Hi you," I say and realize something monumental is about to happen. "How much time do I have?"

"Thirty minutes, you slept with those in your hair?" He points to my old fashioned curlers.

"Ah.... Go! Go in the other room. Don't look at me," I scramble to get the sheet up over my head.

Caleb laughs and walks out, not before saying, "You look cute."

"Ugh! Away!" I threaten.

"Dudette, you're so damn loud. I need sleep," Amber complains. She hops out of bed and runs to the bathroom. "I call dibs on the shower."

"That's cool, I'm in need of a pot of coffee."

"Someone say coffee?" Says the familiar voice.

"Daddy! How did you know to come here?" I throw my arms around his neck trying not to knock the coffee. "I haven't heard from you in over a week. Does mom know you're here?"

He hands me a travel mug full of coffee. This is one thing I miss about him, our morning coffee. "Yes, mom knows I'm here in New Bern. Your grandma and I told her everything last night. She is miffed and scared. Mrs. Ward will take us to the ceremony."

"Just like that," I snap my fingers, "You're OK with me getting married? I don't turn sixteen until Friday. Are you sure this is the right thing to do?"

"Sweetheart, this is right. I can feel the power when I'm with the two of you. Incredible amounts of power. You'll have the power to give me back my light. You can heal me."

"What! I can heal you? How?"

"You're the Queen of all Tamers, it's one of your abilities."

"Can I do it now?" I ask excitedly.

He shakes his head no. "It will need to be done in Fairyland."

"That's amazing, I better go get ready. I'll see you in a while," I say and reach up to kiss him.

Before bed, I packed a duffel bag with things I thought I would need. I brought a sundress and a change of clothes. Grandma told us that we will be home in time for school on Monday. Talk about secrets, I'm a never ending supply of them.

"Ladies, we need to leave," Thorne's voice came from the hallway.

"Give me two seconds to go to the restroom. I'll meet you in the car."

I pick my bag up and start for the door. At the same time, I'm turning the doorknob, my mom is on the other side about to come in the room. We both yelped at the same time.

"You scared me," I say.

"Jessie, I only have a minute. I want to give you something I've had since you were a baby. When I talked to grandma and your dad, it was like a veil was lifted. From the day you were born, I knew there was something magical about you. I don't know how I never figured it out, but I'm glad to know the truth. I'm not going to say that I'm happy they kept this from me for fifteen years. I will say I don't feel any different about you. I love you, and they

are lucky to have you for their Queen. I'm not going to get mushy;
I have something for you. I've had it since you were still in
diapers. I was in Salem, Massachusetts at this quaint antique shop.
It was run by a sweet dwarf couple. She was dressed up in a
witch's costume, playing up the whole witch trial novelty. You
were with me, and I was carrying you on my hip. You were
reaching for everything you could touch. The lady asked me if she
could hold you for a few minutes to let me shop. I was thankful
for the extra hands and took her up on her offer. The minute you
were in her arms, your face lit up with happiness. She commented
how extraordinary you were, most children don't like her. She told
me about holding every child that came into the store, and you
were the first to be entranced with the key. This is the chain she
wore around her neck, and she took it off and handed it to you. I
swore I saw light from your hands, and it made the necklace glow.
The key that was hanging from the chain literally burst with
sparkly lights. The lady smiled and handed me the necklace. She
said to give it to you on your wedding day, for your something old.
She said you'd know what the key is for, so now, I'm giving you
the necklace. Through the years, I've seen that woman everywhere
we've lived. She was never close enough to get a positive I.D. on
her, but I know it was her. If I had to been honest with myself, I
knew your father's drinking was to hide a deep seeded secret. This
is all so much to absorb, but you're not going to be alone. I've
called in to work, and from this day forward, we're not going to
keep secrets."

I took the necklace from her and could feel power vibrating through the metal. I put it around my neck and kissed her.

"Oh, I almost forgot, no one else can touch the key. She was extremely specific about that."

"Okay, come on, the guys are going to come in looking for us if we don't get out to the cars."

The windows of the house were all covered in condensation from the cold air in the house and the humidity outside. The temperature is already ninety, and the sun is four hours away. Parked along the street is about twelve cars with parking lights on. Thorne ran over to grab my bags and took me over to a black Hummer. "Who's in all of these cars? Who's Hummer?"

"Some friends of Mrs Ward, she sent for more guardians and guards to get us safely to the other side. We're not expecting any problems, but we don't want to ignore the possibilities. We'll meet Caleb at the ceremony. Your buddy over there," he points to Amber. "The minute she put her head down, she fell asleep. I've learned she isn't much of a morning person."

"You think? Please tell me we're stopping for coffee. I can't function without an I.V. drip of the caffeine," I say half joking, half seriously.

A man from the front seat reached over and handed me a steaming hot cup of coffee. "Thank you," I say.

"Two sugars and heavy on the creamer, correct Your Highness?"

Here we go with the highness crap. "Thank you, yes that's how I take it." We rode in silence to the trailer we were at yesterday.

Each car had at least two bulky men dressed in black suits. They resembled Secret Service, except younger. We didn't bother going into the trailer, we went straight to the stables. There were so many horses, I didn't bother counting them. Each horse has a rider that looks like they're straight from Medieval times. Outside of the barn is a tremendous carriage covered in flowers. It is one of the old fashioned coaches from western movies. The tufted velvet interior was awkward to scoot across. My inner vampire was dying to put on some fangs and jump out to scare the faeries. I can see Caleb's face if I did something that crazy. Thorne adjusted the ear piece he has in his ear. He told us they were testing it out for the first time on the other side of the shimmer. Not a sound was made by anyone as we took off into the woods.

I start to ask Thorne a question, but he holds his finger to his lips to keep me silent. I cross my arms and sit back on the purple crushed velvet seat. He smiles back at me, and I curled my nose and looked away.

"Onward gentlemen and may the journey be safe and merry," the man who helped us shouted to the riders. The sounds of horses and Amber grinding her teeth are all I hear on the way to the shimmer.

Caleb, can you hear me?

There you are, I tried to get you a minute ago. Are you in that carriage?

I am, but they pulled the drapes down so no one can see inside. This is crazy, huh?

If crazy means you and me, I'll take crazy any day.

Don't let me fall.

Never, I'll always catch you.

I love you.

I love you Jessie Lucentee, my Queen. They're taking me away so you can exit the coach. I'll see you soon. Don't worry, we're not alone.

Bye, my King. I send him a mental hug.

The clearing barely resembled the same place as yesterday. There are flowers wrapped around the trees, as well as long vines of purple flowers. The logs and firepit are gone, replaced by a white gazebo. The clearing is much larger today, but where did all of the trees go? It looked the same but spread out. Faerie magic I'm sure. A massive white tent is set over to the side. I loved all the chairs with white bows on the back. Each table was elaborately set with gorgeous daisy bouquets. Crystal chandeliers floated above the tables. Floated, as in no strings, holy cow!

It wasn't bright outside, but it wasn't dark. It should be darker out, it feels more like dusk.

"Excuse me ma'am, I need to take you to your tent. Is this your lady in waiting?"

I turn around to face the voice, and I'm quite surprised by the little person in front of me. "Lady in waiting? What's that?"

"I forget about you humans, like your maid of honor. She is the one they call Amber, right?" Her voice sounded mechanically altered, too high-pitched to be normal.

"Yes, this is Amber, and I'm Jessie," I hold out my hand to shake hers.

She looks at me and shakes her head. "I'm sorry; I'm not allowed to touch you. My name is Ava, short for Avalon."

"Nice to meet you Ava. Lead the way."

I'm led to a room at the back of the tent, it is sectioned off with wall partitions. Four women come rushing in the room carrying garment bags.

One of the women comes over and asks me to remove my clothes. She fussed about the wedding dress she slaved over for the last few hours. She told me how this is the most notable dress she's ever made.

One of the other women is giving Amber the same speech. They must have gone to disgruntled employee week seminars by the way they acted. My woman wrapped a silk robe around me and took me to the section for make-up and hair.

"I've already done my hair, see my curls?" I say, knowing the curls went to the wayside the moment the humidity hit my hair. I'm not 100% sure she and I speak the same language, and she insisted to pull my hair straight.

After an hour being poked and prodded, the lady slipped the dress over my head. I look over to see my reflection in the full length mirror. The beauty of the pure white silk gown amazed me. I held my breath as I spun around in a circle. It was perfect and beautiful. The wide band that covered my industrial strength bra straps were perfectly placed. The sleeves dipped off my shoulders and gathered right above the elbow. I love how it flows around me as I walk. I couldn't imagine anything more beautiful.

Amber stepped around the corner in a dress similar to mine. It is made of lavender silk and hugs her figure perfectly. She curtsied and held the skirt out to her sides.

"Your highness."

"Your smart-buttness," I replied.

"It's true," she said.

"We have ten minutes."

A familiar voice and face shows up in the doorway. "Ladies, follow me," Thorne says.

I look over to see Amber's jaw is practically on the ground. Who would blame her? His black tuxedo fit him as though he were a Greek god.

I can't help myself, but I feel giddy about the future. I'm ready to heal my dad, and I'm ready to figure out our role here in Fairyland.

"Before we step into the gazebo, there will be two champagne flutes and two small bottles. It is customary for the bride to fill both glasses to show she will serve her husband and their cup will be half full," Thorne says and leads us out of the tent.

"Okay, that sounds sweet, and corny, just my style," I say. The table is covered in flowers and a silk tablecloth. Two amber colored bottles sit next to the crystal champagne glasses. I first one I pick is cold in my hand. I lift it to my nose; its pungent smell almost makes my stomach turn. I hold my breath as I pour the contents into the glass. It bubbled and what looks like little crystals are floating up and down. The next bottle is warmer than the first and the smells are a cross between a greasy burger and maple syrup. I pour it in the other glass and watch as it too creates the bubbles.

Thorne takes my shoulders and turns me around to face the group of people gathered. There weren't any chairs, so everyone was standing around the gazebo.

"I'd like to get everyone's attention," Thorne announces. "Before you, is Jessica Lucentee. The time has come to announce she is to marry Caleb Baldwin. They are two bound Light Tamers that have withstood a break of the bond, yet recovered the bond." A group of people gasped in disbelief. "The Fates have confirmed this union between the two Light Tamers will expose and bring forth the Hidden City of Everlasting Light. If anyone protests this matrimony, a death shadow will be cast over you for the rest of your days." I literally felt everyone hold their breath at the mention of *death shadow.* "Now, if anyone protests may they speak now, or forever hold their tongue." No one said a word. "May the ceremony commence. Mr Lucentee, take your daughter's hand and guide her into the gazebo."

My dad took my left hand and guided me into the gargantuan gazebo. A lovely woman played a gold gilded harp. It was huge against her delicate frame, her slender fingers made the sound magical. My heart was beating in tune with the harp. We stood in the middle in front of a pulpit covered in white daisies that have been weaved into an intricate design. Everything looks and feels beautiful and regal.

I turn to my right, and there he stood. His six foot frame full of muscle filled the black tuxedo. A lavender bowtie around his neck stirred a desire in me I'd never felt before. The way his eyes locked with mine caused my heart to skip two or possibly three full beats. His chiseled cheeks and perfectly trimmed sideburns made him look a little older than his sixteen years. My eyes are drawn to his lips as he mouths the words, *I love you*, to me.

You look so incredibly beautiful. Every time I see you, I can't imagine loving you more, but I do. Believe in us, and everything will work as it should. I promise to never let you fall.

Caleb, I feel the same. I've never imagined a life without you. I'll forever be lost in your eyes and embrace. I promise to always stand tall with you by my side. I love you.

Our moment is interrupted by the clearing of a man's throat. We both laugh shyly as the stranger stares at us.

Caleb do you wonder if they know we can talk without them hearing?

I was thinking the same thing. I don't think they do, and that's just as well.

"EVERYONE," the man shouts so loud I jump and let a squeal. "Hands together. Raise your hands up, showing the unity that binds us as creatures from the earth. We're bringing together two beating hearts and merging them as one." He raises his hands in the air and yells out.

"Go siorai!"

"Go siorai!" The crowd repeats.

I think that means eternally in Gaelic. Caleb thinks to me.

Oh, gotcha.

"Mr Lucentee, do you give your daughter Jessica Aileen Lucentee to Caleb Art Baldwin for the rest of her life?"

"I do," my dad replies and puts my hand into Caleb's hand. "I love you Jess," he whispers and steps back away from me.

A lump starts to grow at the base of my throat.

"Do you Caleb Art Baldwin, take Jessica Aileen Lucente as your wife, to be her forever friend, bound to her heart, and the one and only true love of her life? To love her without questions, cherish and honor her, protect her from chaos and destruction? To soothe her in times of distress and to entwine your heart and spirit?"

Caleb quietly replies, "I do, infinity."

The lump in my throat constricts airflow; the tears welled in my eyes. This is actually happening.

"Do you Jessica Aileen Lucentee, take Caleb Art Baldwin to be your husband, to be his forever friend? To be his partner and his true love? Will you love him without reservation, honor him and trust him, protect him from the perils of life? To soothe him in times of distress and entwine your heart and spirit?"

"I do."

The preacher, which isn't Thorne, who thought he'd be the one to perform the ceremony. This man spoke with authority and absolution with every word. He wore a plain grey suit and black tie. He pulls a rope from the pulpit and holds it above his head. "May the spirits bless this rope to bind the two souls. Will the father of Jessie and Caleb step forward?" I hadn't noticed Mr Gabe, I wonder what he thinks of all of this.

He hands the rope to the men and asks them to tie our wrists together as he repeats a handfasting blessing. "Blessed is this union with gifts from the East. New beginnings with the rising of each sun, in Fairyland. Your heart, mind and body will absorb the nourishment the eastern sun will bring. Blessed be by the gifts of the South. Your heart's passion to warm you in the cold of the winter. Light to illuminate the darkest of times. Blessed be by the West, the cleansing of rain to wash away fears and darkness. Blessed be by the North. Fertility to the fields and to your womb, may they enrich your lives. A stable home to come home to. Take with these the tools of the earth." He sprinkles a handful of dirt over the ropes and rinses it with a cup of water. He holds a ball of light in the palm of his hand and drops it to fall on the rope. Without hesitation, he blows on the light ball. The four elements, of course.

"Do you have the rings?" The man says to Thorne.

He pats his chest and pant pockets, giving a good show of forgetting to bring the rings. I could see the bulge in his pocket as he did his little ruse. Finally, patting the pocket with the box of rings. He hands them to Caleb.

"They are inscribed, please say it out loud for everyone to hear," the man demands.

"Preaditi Unum." Caleb and I say it out loud. Without warning, a sharp pain jabbed me in the heart. By the look on Caleb's face, he has it too.

As quickly as the pain arrived, it was gone. My heart feels strong, yet slower. *"Caleb, what happened?"*

I think our hearts melded together. I think our souls bound together.

"As one, you've been bound by the prophecy. Your rings say, *the gifted one,* and that you are.
As you live as one, you'll die as one or come as close to death as one can. When one heart stops, the other is paralyzed. You'll never be alone if you live and fulfill the prophecy. Now, a test,"

the man says and motions for a waiter to step forward.

The tray with the two champagne flutes is balanced on his hand.

"Caleb, before you are the glasses that represent your union, one is filled with barken-beer and the other with white sumach berry wine. One of the glasses is filled with poison, the other is as harmless as a glass of water. Caleb, you'll be guided by your bride. Jessie, with your hands, bring forth your light and let the light chose."

What do you want me to do? Caleb thought to me.

It's a trick, that is what many of these test things are. One of them smelled sweet, that is the berry. I don't know a lot of white berries to be poisonous, but I'm guessing it is. The pungent one is the barken-beer. I don't know what barken is, but I'm guessing it isn't poisonous. I'll hold my hands over both. I'll pretend to chose one, and you take the other. Are you ready?

I believe in you. Here goes nothing.

Caleb, don't die.

Jess, I'll try.

You're impossible.

We're married, I'm supposed to be.

People are staring.

Okay, my Queen.

The sounds of a horses hooves behind us startle everyone out of silence. A pandemonium breaks out, and we turn around to see what's going on. A stunning blonde woman wearing traditional English riding wear bombarded through the crowd.

"Put that glass down boy. They're both full of poison, any respectable preacher would know better than to pass that trash to royalty." She starts clapping her hands together.

Caleb, do you think she's mad...you know, crazy?

I don't think it, I know it.

"Oh, how darling. What a lovely gown they've made for you. My goodness, what a lovely couple you are. So beautiful, oh to have young love once again. I'm sorry, I forgot to introduce myself. I'm Teagan O'Brian, and around these parts I'm known as the Seelie Queen." She turns her back on Caleb and me to face the crowd. "I am disappointed to find you would go behind my back, and bring forth the supposed Queen of Fairyland and have her marry like a commoner. Why was this hidden from me? Who decided this?"

"I did Teagan, that's who. Now calm your tail-feather and turn to see their first kiss. Their real magic is about to dazzle us all. Come here friend, we'll watch together. Caleb and Jessie, the final piece to the puzzle is for Caleb to kiss his bride."

Beautiful, I'm the luckiest guy on earth and Fairyland. He puts his hand under my chin and steps in closer. Everything around us stops, the melody to my favorite love song from my mom's playlist. Edwin McCain's, I'll Be, is running through my head.

The strands in your eyes that color them wonderful

Stop me and steal my breath

And emeralds from mountains thrust towards the sky

Never revealing their depth.

What is that you're humming? Caleb asks.

Was I humming? It's a song my dad would sing to my mom.

We smiled against each other, lost in the moment. No one watching, no one hearing our thoughts. Until we hear....

"Oh for cripes sake, you become royalty and you subject us to a marathon make-out," Amber teases.

We turn to her and laugh.

"To the people of Fairyland, I introduce you to Caleb and Jessica Baldwin the King and Queen of FAIRYLAND!! Behold the Kingdom of Everlasting Light. All Hail the Light Tamers!" The man who married us announced, very loudly.

"ALL HAIL!" The crowd yells.

Caleb takes my hand. *"Are you ready,"* he asks.

Don't let me fall.

Never.

CHAPTER 23. EQUINOX

"Mom, stop fussing. We're going to be late to the airport. She'll have to get dressed at Caleb's house," I fuss. It's been two weeks since our wedding and nothing, yet everything has changed. We met with the Seelie and Unseelie courts and said we were going to let them to continue ruling the fae. Rumors were spreading at school that Caleb and I got married in a secret wedding because I'm pregnant. Stupid rumors, especially since I have to be a virgin to hold my throne. We felt that rumors are just that, and we wouldn't admit or deny any accusations. It isn't like we're married in the human world.

"Jess, I'll meet you outside. Is Amber staying over tonight?" Mom asked.

I grab my stuff and rush out to the car with her. "No, she's going to dance with Thorne. He got those other guys to come and guard Caleb and me. I still don't know how I'm going to explain the creepy guys that follow us around to Jersey."

Dad is standing outside at the car, holding the door open for my mom. I haven't been able to heal him yet. I tried to put my hands on him and see if it helped. He isn't all the way dark, his desire to steal my light has subsided. Mom and him have been talking on the phone, and have gone to have coffee a few times. I don't know that they'll ever be together as a couple again, but I'm okay with the way it is right now.

"I can't believe you guys let grandma actually chaperone the dance tonight. She's meeting us at the cemetery, the one that Jersey wants to visit before the dance. She said she wants to get pictures by that creepy arch with the wrought iron gates."

"She's always been fascinated with ghosts and cemeteries. She took you walking through one that one time, and you were in hysterics. Do you remember?" Mom laughs at the memory. I can't lie, her laugh makes me laugh. She sounds like a cartoon character when she laughs.

"It was dark," I finally say when I catch my breath from laughing.

Mom laughed. "Oh yeah, I guess that wouldn't be good. I have so much to learn about you Tamers."

"I'm willing to teach you everything I know," dad says flirty to mom.

"Are you now?" She flirts back.

"Oh for the love of all things sacred, I'm the kid," I blurt out. "No flirting."

"Says the Queen." They say in unison.

"Hey dad, I meant to tell you this. Miss Raine had told us she had a girl coming out to talk to us. Her name is Chrissy, and she can heal animals. I guess she can actually talk telepathy with them, and they tell her what is wrong. I've been looking forward to her coming to the class, but she had to cancel. There is some type of Olympic games that are taking place in Ireland. I heard Miss Raine say something about a wolf got hurt. I don't know what kind of Olympic sport has wolves, but I thought that was interesting."

"We'll have to check Google," mom says.

The convention center is decorated with fall themed decorations. We'd eaten cupcakes and hotdogs and tried a few Light Tamer tricks. Amber looked cute in a sassy purple dress with feathers on the hem. No matter how much Thorne tried to deny his feelings for her, the look on his face was obvious.

The DJ called the last dance, and I heard the familiar melody to I'll Be. Caleb held out his hand to me, and I walked with him to the dance floor.

"Mrs. Baldwin?"

"Yes, Mr Baldwin?"

"You look beautiful tonight."

"Oh yeah? You look pretty snazzy too."

He leans over and kisses the tip of my nose.

"What's next?"

"Happily ever after," he whispers in my ear.

"We have to find a way to close the portal," I say. I lean my head against his chest and hear and feel our hearts beating as one.

"It's our destiny, close the portal and stand with these other creatures. We have our first Council meeting next weekend. It's time to bring forth a united front."

"Did I tell you that Mrs Ward had Amber go to her office and told her that her DNA has the code they're hoping will help with the four elements."

Jessie, be quiet about school and stress, let me feel your body dancing next to mine.

Who am I to deny my King? I close my eyes and sway to the music in his arms.

A hand on my shoulder breaks me out of my daydream. "Jess, Caleb, we have trouble. Amber's missing. She went to the bathroom but never came out. I'd been standing on the outside of the door. I didn't hear anything. I went in when she didn't answer me. In red lipstick the name Nyx was written across the mirror," Thorne exclaimed.

EPILOGUE

My bags are all packed, and everything I feel is necessary is in a suitcase or a box labeled Jessie. "Grandma, I don't understand why we have to move to Fairyland. I can't find Amber from there. What if they hurt her or worse, kill her?"

"They would have killed her, and left her for you to find, if that was their motto. It isn't. They want your attention, and they've got it. Time travels different on the other side of the shimmer. We can get you and Caleb trained to seal off the Underworld. It gives you more training days."

"I'm not sealing anything if Amber is in the Underworld. I find her first, dead or alive," I choke as the words come out of my mouth.

"You might not have a choice."

Jessie, we'll find her and bring her home safe.

We can't fail.

Not an option, Caleb says and pulls me closer to him as we ride in the carriage back into the shimmer.

I watched Thorne as he sat quietly lost in his own thoughts as we raced through the forest. He cares more for her than he admits. I can't help but wonder what we're going up against and what sacrifices will be made. I pray she isn't scared. I pray she doesn't get herself into more trouble with that mouth of hers. I smile at the thought of her sassy attitude.

We were able to get Jersey back to New York without her asking too many questions. It was hard trying to reminisce about the Bronx when it isn't all that appealing to me anymore. My home is New Bern. I changed over the summer, and she is still the same. I knew it was the last time I'd see my childhood friend, and close that chapter of my life. After all, I am a Queen.

ABOUT THE AUTHOR

I'll tell you a little about myself (yawn). Devyn is my pen name, my real name is Stefanie. I decided to use a pen name because there is already a Stephenie in the YA world. I write young adult paranormal books about the characters that live in my head. I love reading paranormal books, and love hearing about new authors. I was always considered the 'eccentric girl', the one with the big imagination and colorful stories. Originally, I'm from Oklahoma City…a place I'll always call home. Right now, I live in the lush green and humid climate of New Bern, North Carolina. I was Goth before Goth was a style. I have two adult children that are the be-all-end-all to my life. I have seven pets - 3 dogs, 2 birds and of course my 2 cats.

Thank you to everyone that reads my books. I'm beyond grateful for every review and encouragement from my readers. I'm known for having giveaways on both my blog and my Facebook page. I look forward to hearing from you!

Stalk Me!

The following books are available on Amazon, Barnes & Noble, Smashwords & www.devyndawson.com

www.devyn-dawson.blogspot.com

Twitter - devyndawson

Facebook - Devyn Dawson

MY BOOKS

The Light Tamer

Enlightened - Book Two

Light Bound - Book Three - Spring 2013

If you can't get enough of werewolves - check out the following books by Devyn Dawson

Mature Young Adult

The Legacy of Kilkenny

The Seduction - Novelette -

Malevolence - Book Two - The Legacy of Kilkenny

Sapphire - A Werewolf Love Story - Novella to Malevolence (December 2012)

The Great Wolf - Book Three The Legacy of Kilkenny (March 2013)

Made in the USA
Charleston, SC
29 December 2012